Julie Was Running Through A Nightmare, But It Was All Too Real.

She had to reach the van before the man opened it, led her filly Bonnie out, walked into the trees, took out a gun . . .

The road dipped and swerved away and her light, growing dimmer, barely showed her the direction it took. How far had she run? It must be half a mile now. She could not tell. She only knew she had to get there in time. No hysteria, no panic gave her the wings on her feet: simply love. Her horse was ahead somewhere. In terrible danger. She had to save Bonnie . . .

The Sweet
Running Filly

By PAT JOHNSON
and
BARBARA VAN TUYL

A SIGNET BOOK from
NEW AMERICAN LIBRARY
TIMES MIRROR

SIGNET TRADEMARK REG. U.S. PAT. OFF. AND FOREIGN COUNTRIES
REGISTERED TRADEMARK—MARCA REGISTRADA
HECHO EN CHICAGO, U.S.A.

SIGNET, SIGNET CLASSICS, MENTOR, PLUME, MERIDIAN AND NAL
BOOKS *are published by The New American Library, Inc.,
1633 Broadway, New York, New York 10019*

First Signet Printing, December, 1971

8   9   10   11   12   13   14   15   16

PRINTED IN THE UNITED STATES OF AMERICA

The Sweet
Running Filly

Prologue

SARATOGA

AUGUST

The dawn was a great rising tent-wall of pink gauze behind the low rooftops and Dutch half-doors of the shed row.

A hundred and sixty-five miles to the south lay the largest city in the world—New York, where eight million people were still asleep and you could walk for blocks down the concrete gorges without meeting another soul.

Here, though, among the endless rows of stalls and big clusters of barns that surrounded the racetrack, dawn was a bustle of wide-awake life. Hoofs clopped against hardened ground, the voices of grooms and jockeys echoed back and forth. Bales of hay sailed out to land in the aisles with resounding thuds. The grinding of jaws on brittle oats raised a steady hum of crunching, while those horses still unfed nickered and snorted for their breakfast. Chickens clucked, a lone duck quacked a steady complaint; here and there a dog barked his greeting to the day. Rub rags snapped and fluttered as grooms shook them free of dampness and creases. Currycombs clacked on boot heels, knocking loose the dust that somehow always came out of sleek and glossy coats.

For Leon Pitt, the day began as more than a thousand

other such days had begun, at racetracks all over the country: Belmont, Aqueduct, Keeneland, Pimlico, Churchill Downs, and of course, historic Saratoga itself. Here he'd seen Gallant Fox capture the famous Saratoga Cup, Twenty Grand triumph in the Travers, and Equipoise, "The Chocolate Soldier," gallop to victory in the Whitney Stakes. Wherever a race meeting drew the noblest runners, Leon Pitt was bound to appear, with a twinkle in his eyes, a broad grin on his brown face, and a bucketful of brushes, currycombs, hoof-picks, rub rags, sponges, liniment bottles, and brass sweat scrapers.

Now, once again, he set about his ritual of polishing the horses left in his charge. First one, then another, then another he set to gleaming magnificently with gentle, efficient strokes of his tools. Finally he came to the filly in the last stall at the end of the barn. This yearling was his personal pride. He's raised her mama from a foal, and he'd seen this one into the world himself. Somewhere in the inner folds around her right elbow, in fact, there was the tiny trace of the stitches he had taken after she'd fallen on a rock in the pasture. No one but Leon knew it was there, and aside from that, there was not a marking on her—not so much as a single white hair.

Through the passing months he had watched her woolly baby fuzz transform itself into a deep, rich coat of solid bay. He had noted the sure, steady growth of her limbs, the long, swift strides that one day, he was certain, would make her as great as the best of Thoroughbreds. From a lifetime spent in the company of racers, he knew in his bones that this was going to be a filly to remember.

Even had she promised far less to his expert eye, it was unlikely that he could ever have forgotten her. She was the last remaining Thoroughbred owned by his boss, old Monroe Bradley. As of nightfall, even she would no longer belong in the Bradley stable.

As of nightfall . . . Leon Pitt, too, would no longer belong where he seemed always to have belonged. This day would end as no day had ever ended for him, bringing to a close his career on the turf, his forty years of caring for the Bradley string of racers. Forty years was a long, long time, and a man got to know a lot of things. The thing Leon knew best now was that it was time to quit.

Mr. Bradley had grown old and infirm, unable to keep up an interest in the quality of his stock. Why, the best horse he'd ever bred on the farm was this deep bay filly that Leon was rubbing; and Bradley, his mind no longer alert, barely knew the filly existed. So the family had decided to close down the stable and consign its entire yearling string to the annual Fasig-Tipton sales. The horses had been shipped to Saratoga to be auctioned off in this solid week of bidding.

After the filly, the last of his beloved, four-legged "children," had gone, Leon would retire from racing, to live quietly at home with his human family. For him there'd be no more dawns like this among the sheds of Hialeah, Santa Anita, Narragansett, all the others. There'd be only lazy afternoons of dreaming, of remembering the rare ones, like the filly.

The sun turned the pink sky to light bright blue, burning off the layers of mist and evaporating the dew. The flies began to bite and Flit guns appeared, hissing insect spray up and down the aisles. Then, shortly after noon, the crowd gathered, sifting into the old, elegant tiers of stands, which were thickly bordered with geranium plantings and nestled among trees that had stood there when Horatio Gates had whipped the British of Gentleman Johnny Burgoyne at the second battle of Saratoga. Here the cream of the sporting rich gathered with entire stables of Thoroughbreds to race; with family fortunes to spend buying more; and with a certain number of hustlers waiting around for the usual crumbs—small change for minor favors, an invitation to a social event, or a cast-off horse, perhaps gone lame.

The afternoon passed in a breathtaking sequence of photo finishes, blazing stretch drives, and fat purses of coveted prize money. The crowd had enjoyed a really good day of racing. Now, Leon knew, they'd be ready for spending on this last and biggest night of the annual week-long yearling auction that was the high point of the season.

After dinner, the bidders convened in the Fasig-Tipton auction pavilion. They had assembled, of course, for no ordinary horse sale. This was a dress occasion, as closed to the public as a fashionable drawing-room social affair, as formal as a private banquet. Dark, beautifully cut suits moved among long, shimmering gold and silver gowns; names such as Whitney, Vanderbilt, duPont glittered in the conversation like the gems on the fingers, wrists, and throats of the ladies. Everyone knew everyone else. Only the horses were lonely.

Lost and bewildered, away from home for the first time in their lives and each headed nobody knew where, many hadn't even a proper name. They were merely numbers on tags pasted to their flanks—hip number such-and-such now brought before the bidders. No wonder each one felt forlorn.

Whinnies and neighs cried out in the darkness and Leon Pitt had all he could do to keep his filly from blowing sky-high in the walking circle among the others waiting their turn. At last he heard the attendant call, "Hip number 282, bring her up, please!"

Leon led the filly through the bypass, lined with trainers and grooms, and on to a small roped-off stage in the center of a horseshoe of chairs and bidders. All the while he flourished his rub rag, working even more shine into the lustrous coat that already dazzled with mahogany glints. The gavel cracked on the speaker's desk; sounding intensely bored, the auctioneer began a description of the filly. The audience was hushed, for this was the animal they had awaited. She fidgeted and jigged in a circle, straining against Leon's firm hold. In confusion, in dread of this strange place with its throng of humans stirring in the gallery, she nickered softly. It sounded like a whimper, and Leon flinched with pity.

"Ladies and gentlemen, the Fasig-Tipton yearling dispersal now offers for your consideration hip number 282—a most rare individual whose quality and lineage are without parallel! Look at her, ladies and gentlemen! By Bold Ruler, four times Horse of the Year and leading money-winner of all time, out of the hundred percent producer Starcrossed, herself a stakes winner of over half a million dollars! Starcrossed, by the imported Princequillo, an amazon in her own right . . ." Leon tried to soothe the filly, to reassure her, as the superlatives droned on. ". . . won sixteen races and placed in her only defeat under top weight and running with colts!"

The auctioneer paused for emphasis, then continued. "She has three other foals of racing age. All are stakes winners. Her first foal, Starless Night, winner of the Coaching Club Oaks . . ." The racing particulars were many, but Leon knew that just one look at the filly would tell any real judge of horses that she was class. Finally, "And here she is, ladies and gentlemen, in the family of Starless Night, Deep Wonder, and Northern Lights—with the potential to eclipse them all!"

His recitation ended, a brief thick hum rose from the gallery, as buying agents consulted their clients on how high they were authorized to go. Silence returned as the auctioneer started the bidding.

". . . will begin at seventy-five thousand dollars. Do I have eighty-fi . . . nine . . . ninety-fi . . ." The words had barely begun before the price had leaped to $150,000.

"Ladies and gentlemen!" The gavel struck sharply. "Let us not dicker in these paltry sums for an individual so magnificent as you see before you tonight. Let's get down to serious buying. Now, who'll give me—" he paused for an instant—"who'll give me exactly two-unerd-ousen-ollars?" He rushed the words together as though two hundred thousand were a trifle unworthy of the time it took to pronounce it.

Several hands flickered swiftly. Here and there a head nodded a solemn agreement. At least a dozen buyers were willing to meet this awesome price.

The figure mounted rapidly. Ten thousand more here, another ten there, another, still another.

"Yessir," said the auctioneer somewhat uneasily. "From Mr. Phipps' agent we have a bid of three hundred thousand dollars." He pronounced the words slowly and loudly. Even to him, this was a towering sum of money. Under cover of a sudden surf of voices from the gallery, he whispered to a nearby assistant.

"This bidding's crazy for an untried horse, I don't care *how* she's bred! We knew she'd bring a terrific price, but this is out of hand! She's four thousand over the record now—"

"And if, heaven forbid, she turns out to be a lemon—" said the other man.

"The publicity would tighten the purse strings of every future buyer we ever had. Do what you can to discourage the bidding, Jim, and I'll do my best to conclude this sale. Fast!"

He dabbed nervously with his handkerchief at the sweat gleaming on his face. He waved the gavel. "I have three hundred thousand once, three hundred twi . . ." A kind of genteel agitation spread through the crowd, and the lighted board behind the stand was a jumble of changing numbers racing to keep up with the onrush of bids. At last they came to rest, an unheard-of $325,000. In the moment of shocked quiet that followed, a cool voice said from the edge of the crowd, "Three hundred and fifty thousand dollars."

The auctioneer was sweating faster than before. The gallery rustled in a new surge of excitement. "Ladies and gentlemen I ah have uh three hundred and ah fifty thousand, now surely this——"

His plea was stopped in mid-stammer. "Three seventy-five," shouted someone from the center, a note of disgust in his tone. Once again the gallery whispered and sighed and gasped with amazement, with disbelief.

"Three hundred seventy-five," the auctioneer repeated. No longer could he conceal his nervous despair. He gripped the gavel as if he intended to squeeze it into splinters, and said huskily, "Ah, shall we conclude this uh———"

"Four hundred thousand dollars." It was the cool voice over at the edge of the throng.

The gavel banged down with determination. Enough was enough. "I have four hundred thousand once." He was not wasting a second. "Four hundred thousand twice." Briskly, before they realized his haste on the very heels of the unprecedented amount, the wooden mallet pounded out its final crash. "Four hundred thousand dollars . . . SOLD!"

Leon's eyes searched the crowd for the man who'd made the final bid, but he was now lost in the swelling confusion.

"SOLD! To Mr. Tolkov of Deepwater Farm for *four hundred thousand dollars.*"

The stunning words were lost in the uproar. The filly neighed in high, piercing screams and tried to wheel and bolt from the platform. Leon set his weight full against the lead shank and steadied her back into control. "Come on, Gum Drop," he whispered to her gently. "Ain't nothing bad gonna happen to you, old girl. Now get your feet back on the ground an' act like the proper lady you was born. That's right, Gum Drop, that's my good old Gum Drop. Right along with me." He patted her neck and smoothed her mane as they ambled together back to the barn. He put her in the stall, gentled her for a few moments, started to leave, then gazed back for one long quick endless breath of time.

Good-bye, Gum Drop. Good-bye, shed row. Good-bye, racing.

Good-bye, horses. Good-bye, you one best sweet little horse.

Chapter 1

It was June. Standing at the store window, Julie Jefferson gazed absentmindedly at the rain. It fell steadily, the sort of rain that persuades old people sitting on front porches in small towns to fold their newspapers, collect their knitting, pick up their pokes of peppermints, and go indoors for the rest of the day. No use, thought Julie, to stare at that raw gray sky and mutter farmers' wisdom about clouds soon blowing over south toward Amityville, or flash floods washing out bridges and rising so many inches over last year's prize downpour. This was a businesslike, middle-of-June rain, obviously intended purely for irrigation. When the earth was wet enough, it would stop; until then the prophecies of mere human beings would have no effect on it whatever.

Julie watched the big drops coursing down the glass. Idly she wondered: Before the weather breaks, won't every soul in Blankton, Ohio, stand dreamily at some other window, seeing other drops of rain strike, cluster, quiver, trickle away in streaks? Maybe water has a faint hypnotic force, fleetingly holding anyone with the spell of its rhythms and designs . . .

The golfer, irresistibly following the arc and sweep of a sprinkler's geyser on the green. The fisherman, rapt by concentric ripples that signal the impact on still water of almost invisible insects. The small boy, un-

14

aware of his aloneness as he squats on a curb to watch small cataracts roil and rise and turn the gutter into a bubbling brown river. And who was it, now—Bet-A-Million Gates?—the colorful gambler she'd read about, who wagered some fantastic amount that one raindrop would beat another down a windowpane from top to ledge? As if they'd been Thoroughbreds. as if he'd known their pedigrees and track records!

Circling behind the cash register, she moved to the crystal and china. Methodically, she lifted each fragile piece, smoothed away the dust with her cloth and set it back. Next she'd come to her favorite display, the antique collection of military miniatures—toy soldiers, really, no matter what Dad called them. They were probably not much more than fifty years old, but that certainly made them antiques to her.

Here the armies of Europe were assembled, dressed in the uniforms of 1812: muskets, lances, swords, cocked hats and bearskins, cavalry and infantry poised on parade or readied for assaults that would never be ordered. How excited her father had been the day he'd made this find! Together they'd pored over military histories, prints, engravings, paintings of the Napoleonic period, carefully researching color, equipment, and costume. Then at last he'd mixed his paints and polished his magnifying lens, trimmed the tiny sable brushes, sharpened the fine-bladed knives, and begun to restore the troops to their original brilliance. His hands moved in small, precise strokes, returning luster to leaden swords, replacing epaulets knocked off long ago, tracing delicate hairline gold braid and fancy frogging, correcting the dulled and haphazard original painting until the little men were made whole again, and more accurate than they had ever been before. The cavalry mounts he saved for last, and magically turned them with shadowed muscles and freshly arched necks into real horses that seemed to breathe and snort. The horses, of course, Julie liked best of all the splendid display . . .

There was nothing her father could not fix, it seemed

to her. Including damaged living things. The pair of tawny retriever puppies, hit by a car down the road; the cat whose paw had been stabbed by a pitchfork; the calf badly mangled by barbed wire—they'd all left his gentle hands cured and happy. And especially there was the baby raccoon.

Julie had discovered it in a trap in the woods. Its hind legs had been crushed by the snapping steel and it lay at her feet in a matted wad of blood and fur, too weak to stir as she bent to pry the metal jaws apart and free it. Only its eyes moved when she touched it, two big glazed stones rimmed in black. In cycles of pain and desperate fright they opened, widened, fixed her in focus, dulled and closed, then opened and repeated the pathetic stare and closing.

So very gentle she tried to be, and hated her hands for their clumsiness; but she gathered up the sad little bundle and raced home with it to her father.

No need to explain or plead for help! He opened the kitchen door and in the same motion reached out for the poor creature that she laid in his hands. A heartbeat later he was listing the things he needed, and her own frantic misery was changing to a fearless, orderly calm as she followed the murmured orders and produced cotton, warm water, gauze, surgical tape, antiseptic, scissors . . . His fingers moved with dexterity and love. The animal watched him without moving, but now, it seemed to Julie, it was not so much paralyzed with terror as beginning to relax with a strange new trust in this incredible gentleness. When the whole ordeal was over and the baby had drunk some water greedily and, stitched and taped together, was actually beginning to test the makeshift splints, Julie paused to consider the special gifts of her father. Was it the skill of those hands that made such healing possible, or was it the profound, spontaneous tenderness that no living thing could fail to sense in his touch?

Whatever it was, the poor maimed beast had recovered, had turned into the most affectionate adolescent raccoon on record, and having absolutely refused its freedom, now lived with them in a state of friendly rivalry with the two fully grown retrievers. Occasionally it would mooch off to the woods for a day or so, but it always came back to Julie—and especially to her father.

In the presence of someone so gentle, so loving, so overjoyed with the simple adventures of life as her father, Julie could not imagine doing anything less than trying to be the best person she could be. This was why she was often so amused when adults praised her as a "model daughter," or cooed about her behavior as an "exemplary child." They carried on as though she were a saint, when the fact was that she just plain *enjoyed* her father. Being with him was more fun than hanging around with a whole pack of kids her own age.

She set down the last horse—a big drummer's gray, two and a half inches long—moved to a window and opened it, stuck out her hand and briskly snapped the dusting cloth, the way she'd seen Stash, the groom at St. Clairs, pop his rub rag. She had to get moving; Dad would be fidgeting to start the antique expedition. If she were much later than noon, he'd think she'd had some customers. It would disappoint him, though he wouldn't show it, to find that she'd only been daydreaming about raindrops and toy horses.

Julie looked forward to the trip. She liked auction sales, and poking about in little quaint shops that were going out of business, and visiting in modest homes where hardworking folk could no longer afford to let great-grandfather's clock or desk collect dust in the attic. Best of all were the infrequent journeys to elegant mansions, where whole collections of exquisite treasures might be purchased. It was not sad at all, rich people parting with heirlooms, because they had many other things to cherish, probably too many to look at more than once a year. And on an estate there would likely be horses.

Julie Jefferson would have driven, or walked, three miles past the ends of the earth to find a horse. Just to discover a horse to *be with* for a while. To stand with her arm thrown over a horse's neck was all she required for total contentment. Under Stash's tutoring she'd become a better-than-average rider, yes; but riding in itself wasn't the key to that extraordinary sensation of fulfillment that welled up inside her when she could share a few moments of companionship with a horse.

Most people, she'd discovered, couldn't grasp the nature of this affinity. The common belief was that you loved horses because you loved riding. But Julie's emotions worked the other way round. She loved riding because she loved horses. Sitting astride a horse was just one expression of the closeness of two spirits, no more and no less satisfying than playing together in a grassy pasture, nuzzling in a warm, dark stall, hand-walking after a bath to dry out, or grooming on a pair of crossties snapped across a stable aisle.

She closed the cash register, snapped the front latch, and walked through the tidy office to the rear of the store, where her worn rain slicker hung limp above shiny black rubber boots, tops flopped sideways almost to the floor. She slipped off her loafers and dragged on the boots, grinning at a thought. Her father's cautious rule about bolting up tight against burglars always amused her. Was there a single self-respecting thief anywhere, she wondered, who'd choose Blankton as a target? And what would Bonnie and Clyde, or Raffles, do with such unwieldy loot as filled Jefferson's Gift and Antique Emporium, Randolph Jefferson, II, Prop.? Blankton's most positively unthriving store, stuffed with Queen Anne chairs, Empire tables, Scottish grandfather clocks, pseudo-Tiffany chandeliers, and the largest known collection of refurbished turn-of-the-century toy soldiers.

No, Julie told herself as she shrugged on her slicker and lifted her long blond hair from beneath the collar, that sign on the margin of town is definitely wrong. *Welcome to Blankton, Town of Law-Abiding Citizens.*

It should really be corrected: *Welcome to Blankton, Town with Nothing Anyone Wants to Steal.*

She eased out the back door into the rain, which seemed to be letting up a little. She scurried across the dirt pull-in driveway to "Bearcat," the indestructible, ancient, green pickup truck that they used for errands and rough work. Idling the engine for a minute because of the pervading dampness, she then backed down the drive, checked the nonexistent traffic, cornered onto the road, shifted and throbbed and thunked off down Route 9—Main Street. She hadn't had her license very long and was still conscious of being grown up each time she slid behind the wheel.

Well, come to think of it, now that I'm out of high school (even if it is *barely* out of high school) I s'pose I am pretty much grown up.

It was not a smart-alecky thought. Julie did not consider herself super-educated, worldly wise, as mature as a middle-aged matron and quite equipped to run the country. But it did begin to occur to her, as she passed the white frame houses and the ten or twelve stores that made up the town, that as of last week's graduation exercises, she alone was accountable for the kind of person she became, the kind of life she forged. College was out of the question. Her marks had been excellent, her teachers had urged her to apply for a scholarship, but her father would be desolate without her and leaving him was a prospect she had long ago dismissed.

So now there were no teachers to rescue, mold, advise, enlighten her. There were no daily classes to offer ready-made the ingredients of life—friends, ideas, regrets, annoyances, opinions, fun . . . She must now construct for herself the life she'd lead, with no one but her father to count on for help in this enormous project. She was on her own, with nowhere to go but Blankton; that realization was not exactly comfortable.

Her thoughts inched closer to the area she didn't

want them to touch. She concentrated fiercely on her driving, but the question was there now.

What if Mother were still alive?

What if Flight 607 from Boston to Columbus had not plummeted into the Atlantic three years before graduation? If it had only landed safely somewhere on this earth, and returned to Dad and me that dear, kind, gentle presence who made us a home, a love, a great irreplaceable warmth? I'd have different plans, yes, be doing other things; but would I myself be different?

There'd be college, Julie reflected, perhaps even a veterinarian's degree and pursuit of the dream of her childhood, a breeding station and medical center exclusively for horses. But more, much more, there'd be no dreadful double loneliness, hers and her father's. There'd never have been that brutal sorrow to yank the luxury of lingering childhood right out from under her, nor that fist of despair under her nose threatening her to hurry and grow up, chasing her toward adulthood till she arrived at some serenity to ease the passage of days and nights.

Indeed, she asked herself, if Mother were here, would I be my same self, or would some better, confident stranger have grown beneath my skin?

A horn blasted out behind her. With a start, she saw that a red light had just turned green without her noticing.

"Pushy creep," she said quietly, shifting and pulling off down the road. The intrusion of the impatient motorist helped to shoo her thoughts from sadness; the dismal weather was enough to fight, without dwelling on what-might-have-been.

The faithful pickup rattled through the charmless outskirts of Blankton, where diners, billboards, and an occasional (and illegal) dump made their crawling assaults on the road. Bearcat's chassis vaulted on its springs, smacked down again, lurched and bucked like a fat unbroken pony as it passed over a stretch of super-bumps and potholes that signaled the approach of her turnoff, just past the red-and-blue-lettered sign that advised her of her wonderful luck at having her taxes hard at work rebuilding this road.

"Oh wow," she said to Bearcat, patting it gently on its scarred old dashboard. "Hope twitches eternal. They're going to widen the bumps for us and run a groovy divider between the craters."

She steered carefully across the slippery road and onto the mud-streaked macadam of the farm route that led home. In seconds she was beyond the ugliness of the advertising and thoughtless earth-pollution. Now, as far as the eye could penetrate beneath the low gray clouds, was almost nothing but greens: the rosy purple green of clover, new buds rearing above the grass, the ash and honey green of hay fields where ripening tips of alfalfa and timothy swayed heavily on their stalks awaiting early harvest, the flat milk-green of used pasture interrupting great reaches of deep, rich, untouched bluegrass. Lines of fence, four panels high and darkened almost black from creosote and weather, appeared and vanished along the rolling land, finally settling into a miles-long border on each side of the road.

Then the fencing broke to show, between a pair of stone pillars, a well-kept rambling gravel drive. Set into each column was a bronze plaque informing her, as if she didn't know, that this was St. Clair Farm.

Julie peered through the slap and swish of the wipers. From habit she scanned the meadows, half hoping to see some dear, familiar face nuzzling its mother, half relieved to find that, as she'd expected, Stash had pulled them in, away from the raw rain.

The mares would be nestled in their stalls, hovering over foals that could barely wobble through the thick mounds of straw on legs still spindly and teetering. Thank goodness, tomorrow's Sunday, she thought; I'll beat it out of the house by dawn and be down at the barn to help Stash feed. It had been an eternity, not just six days, since the last Sunday—the only full day she had off now to spend at the St. Clair barns.

The meadows were halted soon by a dense wood, the raccoon's wood, which seemed to be owned by no one and had sat there growing thicker and wilder for as long as anyone could remember. Beyond it were a couple of small dirt farms, plowed and planted with the coming summer's yield of vegetables. Then Julie slowed the truck and tooted a warning to possible oncoming cars as she mounted to an old single-lane stone bridge and crossed the creek high-swollen with rain.

She remembered suddenly the ad in yesterday's paper that had prompted her father and her to plan this afternoon's expedition:

SPIRE'S ORIGINAL YARD
"You Name It, We Got It"
Livestock   Farmgoods   Firewood
Auto Parts—Plumbing Fixtures
Rare Antiques
&
Junque
2 Miles North of Amityville

It sounded like a possible hunting ground, all right. But why did Julie's scalp prickle as she recollected the ad? Maybe, she told herself, grinning, some witch in a bog, a thousand years back in my ancestry, is telling me we'll find a priceless treasure!

More likely, she's telling me that I should wear a scarf over my hair when it's raining and cold and miserable!

Chapter 2

On the far side of the bridge was home: a weathered shingle farmhouse, no longer attached to a farm, but comfortably set amid the Jeffersons' few acres of woodland, orchard, and lawn—a lawn that needed mowing. Julie turned sharp right and swung up the drive and right into the old red cowshed that now served as shelter for Bearcat and the fairly late-model car.

She switched off the engine and instantly heard the *whap* of the screen door springing shut. Here came the two taffy-coated retrievers, fully grown and obviously healthy, bounding out through the rain.

"Hey, Cissy love, hey, Joey! You guys shouldn't be out in the rain," she shouted, opening the truck door. Suddenly her lap was full of wet fur and muddy paws, her hands and cheeks sloshed with the wild slap of tongues and frantic whip of tails. "You're all moist," she laughed, embracing them. "You're *damp!*"

"And so are you, miss," said a stern voice at the entrance. Rand Jefferson stood there against the gray daylight, hands on hips, trying to imitate a mean parent whose child had disobeyed him once too often. It was a perfectly awful imitation, thought Julie, and giggled as he came forward and she saw the pleasure dancing in his blue eyes and the uncontrollable smile twitching up the ends of his neat gray mustache. "If I've said it once, I've said it thirteen thousand and eight times.

Keep a wet dog in its place. Which is not your lap. Two soppy, floppy hounds are enough, not to mention a rain-soaked raccoon, without having a dripping, half-drowned daughter—" He shook a long brown finger under her nose. "Without any headgear, too." He took off his sou'wester, which matched his ancient oilskin raincoat, and jammed it down over her head.

"Pray do not terrify me so," said Julie, floundering through the chaos of dogs to the floor of the shed. She reached up and gave him a kiss on the jaw. "You know what a timid child I am."

"Forgive my terrible temper," he said. "Did you eat any lunch? There's a large sandwich on the kitchen table, and a thermos of milk. If you'll take these two dissolving mutts indoors, I'll get the car warmed up. Burglar's asleep under the stove.

She plunged out into the rain, the retrievers doing their best to trip her; they always seemed to feel that she should be running on all fours with them. The screen slammed behind them. Julie gathered up her lunch, patted the dogs farewell, glanced under the old stove and saw the raccoon's eyes glowing sleepily at her, went outside and locked the door, hearing Joey and Cissy howl in outrage at being left behind. She paddled through mud puddles to the garage. She got into the car and began to eat her sandwich as they pulled away on the journey to Amityville.

For a while they speculated together on what they might discover at Spire's Original Yard. ("It must be several thousand years old," said Rand thoughtfully, "if it's the original.") Then they sang songs, until "The Old Gray Mare" reminded Julie of horses, and they settled down for twenty miles or so to speak of her abiding passion: of big horses, little horses, show horses, plow horses, racehorses, trotting horses, walking horses, war-horses, and just plain horses. Luckily for her, Julie thought, her father was very fond of them too—though probably no one in the universe could match her own obsession with them!

As they drew near to Amityville, and began to

watch for the Yard, conversation died. At last, two miles short of the village, as the advertisement had said, a weathered sign announced that their destination was A Hunnert Feet to the Left.

"Hand-painted by Spire's Original Three-year-old Son," murmured Julie.

"In the dark," added her father, who immediately reproached himself aloud for making fun of someone simply because they weren't too skillful at spelling.

"Sorry," said Julie, contrite.

"Me too," said Dad.

They turned in through what had become a slight drizzle and bounced over the Original Mud Road for some hundreds of feet. The Yard lay before them. Julie was appalled.

"Oh wow!" she said, blinking.

"For once, I agree with that peculiar expression," said Rand Jefferson blankly.

The term "shambles" did not convey half the disorder that met their eyes. Spire's place was about one stiff breeze away from total collapse. The house itself, from which the clutter spread outward like some creeping infection, resembled the setting of an extremely run-down ghost story; but no self-respecting ghost would have been caught dead—or alive, or whatever—inside its four paintless, rickety walls. A gray and almost formless shed leaned weakly westward; its mate a little way off bent toward the east. Spilling out of the doors, as well as from holes in the sides where boards had long ago quit trying to hold on, tangles and heaps of metal things that Julie could not identify rusted in red-brown confusion. Under a canvas tent, tied with cords to a dead sapling, rested exactly one half of a harrow, minus its teeth. Piles of parts for unknown machines, several refrigerators ("Dating from the Punic wars," thought Julie), crippled clocks and spavined chairs, three-legged tables and no-legged tables, uncounted stacks of firewood that you'd have had to clean with ammonia or turpentine before putting onto your hearth, automobile parts plainly rejected by some scrap-metal drive—the list was endless, and each item less decorative, more useless, than the last.

Far worse, though, were the animals. As Julie scanned the place, her stunned amusement gave way to real horror. Was this awful Yard run by a human being? And where was the local authority in charge of preventing cruelty to such poor beasts as these?

The pigs, at least, looked reasonably fit. Grunting, jamming their noses into the rubbish, they were plump enough and not much dirtier than the usual farm pig. But the cattle were like grotesque hat racks covered thinly with secondhand hides, on which most of the spots were their own filth; their heads hung wearily and it plainly took all their strength to stand up in the muck and the jagged junk that constantly threatened their poor tottery legs.

The barnyard fowls were scrawnier than any Julie had ever seen before. They were like survivors of a war, existing somehow on this scorched earth, too feeble to flap their wings, too weak to cluck or crow, too discouraged to peck.

Julie yearned with all her soft and sentimental heart to pack up every chicken, cow, and duck on the place and take them home for a wash, a good meal, and a few hugs apiece to let them know that all mankind wasn't as thoughtless—or cruel—as the critter who owned this dreary, evil place. Barring that . . .

"Let's not get out," she said to her father, voice shaking in spite of clenched teeth. "Let's go report him to the police or somebody."

"It looks worse than it is, honey, because the rain's made the lot of 'em muddy and bedraggled. You can't tell, there just *might* be something worth buying; I doubt if antique collectors visit here on a regular basis." Rand shut off the motor and opened his door. "Maybe we'll rescue a chicken or two," he said kindly, seeing the sickness in her eyes.

Julie slowly got out. She knew they couldn't take on any more pets, and you couldn't have eked out enough from any one of these flimsy fowls to make a respectable pot of soup. She walked over through the clutter to smooth the ruffled feathers of a hen, which cocked a wary eye at her. As though she were going to kick it! she thought. Oh, this was a terrible, a *wicked* place!

A man came out of the moldering house and waddled toward them. He was about five feet high and three feet wide, with more lard on him than any of the pigs had. "Oh towering Spire," whispered Rand, in a vain effort to cheer up his daughter. He nodded curtly then and said, "You advertise, ah, rare antiques?"

"You a dealer?" asked Spire. His voice was a trickle of molasses over gravel. "I got some mighty fine stuff inside the house." He waved a pudgy hand that had been washed no later than last Wednesday. "You want to look around out here first?"

"I have," said Rand Jefferson. He started to follow Spire toward the odd piece of architecture, then glanced back at Julie and said, "Coming, honey?"

"I think I'll explore." She didn't want to be any closer to the unpleasant man than she could help. And maybe she could locate some tender grass to feed to the unhappy cows.

She picked her way between rusted bedsprings and a rooting sow, heading for the rear of the property where between the trunks of round-topped catalpa trees she could glimpse a distant expanse of green. Then she saw it.

She could not believe that it was what it seemed to be. No, oh no . . . It was a specter, and just the sort of horrid, pitiful ghost that *would* haunt a place like Spire's Yard. It couldn't be real.

She let out a yelp of sympathy and dismay. Of course it was real.

It was a real, live, suffering horse.

Ignoring the danger of sharp rusty iron and slippery muck, she ran toward it, never realizing that she was crying aloud to it as she went.

"Hold on, I'm coming! Hang tough, boy!"—one of

her father's favorite orders, always delivered (as she did now) in a tone of affection.

All she could see was its head at first, though from the jerks and tossings of that head she knew that the beast was tied and terrified. It was beyond the yard itself and its body was hidden by rising ground. It was not making any sound whatever, only throwing itself back and forth with weak violence. It did not seem to have as much padding on its skull as even the pathetic cattle.

Stumbling up the rise, Julie saw a sight that she was to witness again and again in her nightmares. The horse was not standing in a little valley, as she'd imagined.

It was submerged to the shoulders in a dirty brown river.

A corroded wire cable stretched sagging from one bank to the other, fastened with great iron staples to an oak tree on either side. Hooked to this cable was a heavy, rusted chain. The chain was wired to the throat latch of an old, rotting halter on the animal's head. The chain was much too thick and too long for its job, and had been tangled by the horse's frantic spasms of movement until it was a red mass of knots and jagged loops about the head and throat. Some of the red was rust and some was blood.

Before the chain had become fixed where it was, it must have lashed freely and viciously, for the withers and shoulders of the horse were striped here and there with lines of blood. Patches of hide had been torn from the face and neck. If Julie had had Mr. Spire there at that instant, she would have hurled him into his own river and sat on his head.

"There, there, poor baby, stand easy, I'm coming," she said, and without a thought of her own safety, slid down the bank and waded out into the filthy water. A yard from the bank she stepped on a wet rock and sat down heavily with a splash. Her concern for the horse was so strong that she didn't even say *ouch,* although it hurt. She scrambled up somehow and went forward, talking gently and making small calming motions with her hands. She was absolutely shaking with rage and pity.

The horse eyed her. It was a young animal, a bay Thoroughbred, so thin and frail-looking that it reminded Julie of nothing so much as the dying in a nerve-shattering picture she'd seen in art class, a distressing thing called "Guernica" by Picasso, which she'd never been able to erase from memory. The once-beautiful hide was drawn taut over the good bones, the flesh so meager that it was a wonder the horse had strength to thrash around in the water. As she neared it, it showed her the whites of its eyes and backed off to the limit of the chain, snorting weakly.

"No, no, pretty horse, dear little horse, I wouldn't hurt you," Julie soothed it, approaching very slowly. "I want to help, I want to take that shackle off you, dear." All the compassion in her voice, she thought, was no substitute for the assurance her father would have projected if he'd been there; why, the horse would have been coming to *him* by this time.

Maybe by the time I'm thirty or so, I'll be able to talk to animals so they really know how I feel. And handle them with—with skill and love.

Well, I have the love now, for heaven's sake. Let me show it.

She might have run back for her father, but there wasn't time, there seemed to be no time at all in which to save this woeful beast. She moved forward to stand beside it in the opaque water, which was up almost to her waist. It pulled its head high and rolled its eyes down at her, blowing between soft, cut lips.

"Don't be afraid," she said as evenly as possible, "I'm just going to set you free."

She couldn't do that, naturally. The horse wasn't hers to release. She'd probably go to jail!

It might be worth it. It would be worth it.

She reached up slowly, but not too slowly, and tried to untangle the worst of the chain's knots, which reached from cheek to muzzle. It gashed her fingers, but she was unaware of any pain. The horse stamped in the water and jerked its head nervously. After what felt like ten minutes—it might have been one—the links were disentangled. Julie put her hand firmly on the long bony face and after a short struggle the horse lowered its head. At the same time it shifted suddenly to the near side and stepped on her foot. Julie skidded and lost her balance and sat down for the second time. She was now sopping to the ears.

Lucky I was on mud and not rock, she said to herself, getting to her feet slowly so she wouldn't alarm the animal. Her toes hurt. She didn't care. Patiently she brought the head down again and pulled one loop of the hideous chain up and off. The horse looked at her with wide eyes. For a moment she stood without moving, staring back into the big brown orbs. They were the most alive parts of the whole piteous creature. There was intelligence glowing in their depths, and something more, a dampened but still bright flame of spirit.

"Oh, there's a good horse," she said gently, "there's a brave smart little horse." She took another length of the chain from the neck and carefully brought it down past the ears and eyes, protecting them with her free hand, and the horse stood steady. *"Such* a fine horse," she murmured, over and over, freeing it link by link from several snarled lumps of chain. At last it was done. She smoothed the cut neck, barely touching the hair, as she wondered what to do next. The chain hung heavily from the rotten halter, more than half of it under water.

She couldn't just take off the halter and allow it to run away. That was criminal—not as criminal as keeping it here, certainly, but still very much against the law—and besides, the poor thing would only be killed on the highway, or die of its wounds and mal-nutrition. But . . . but . . .

"Think you can shorten that chain without tools?"

Julie whirled around, startled, and nearly fell in the

river again. Her father was squatting on the bank
watching her.

"I think so."

"Back in a minute," he said, and walked off toward
their car. She gazed after him. He had looked at her
oddly; she couldn't decide what that expression on his
tanned face had meant. Surely he wasn't angry with
her for getting wet? No, not Dad. What, then?

She moved through the hampering water, away from
the horse which was standing quietly, its head drooping,
and examined the fastening of the chain and cable.
The chain ended in an enormous clasp, a releasable
catch the spring of which was corroded nearly in two,
but still bent stiffly under the pressure of her fingers.
She picked up the heavy chain and gauged the best
possible span. The horse should be able to reach the
water to drink, perhaps even to lie down in the
shallows; she made sure that the clasp slid with some
ease along the old cable. She heaved the weight over
her head and shoved a link across the rusty spring
into the loop of the catch. Then, so that the horse
would not tangle itself in the extra chain, she made a
double loop by forcing a second link into the clasp.
Now the horse could injure itself on the chain only by
walking into the double garland of iron, which it wasn't
likely to do. She made certain once more that the
fastener still would move on the cable. The horse had
raised its head and was watching her with a kind of
feeble, pathetic interest. She laid her wet cheek against
the solid bay cheek and crooned to it without words.
The long head moved away and then returned to touch
her with its nose, the briefest, softest of kisses.

"Why, you *know*," Julie said, amazed. "You know
I wanted to help. Oh, you smart little thing!" And
without meaning to, she burst into tears. She would
have hugged it, but it was so hurt and vulnerable even
to caresses.

"Hey," said Rand Jefferson. "Come here and take
this."

She floundered ashore, sniffling. "This" was a tin of

Furacin ointment. "Where'd you get it?" she asked stupidly.

"Always carry it in the glove box. In case. You put it on that poor cuss while I go buy a clock from Spire." He was still observing her with unreadable expression.

"Hadn't you better do it? You're so much better at it than I am."

"No sense of both of us dripping all over the car, honey," he said shortly, and turned away.

He must be mad at me. But he doesn't *quite* look mad.

She returned to the animal and began to apply the salve cautiously to the raw spots, gashes and chain bruises on face, neck, breast, and shoulders. The horse backed away, uneasy, and several times threw up its head restively as she touched a painful place, but it did not once offer to nip her, which was little short of miraculous. Gradually she gained confidence—not in the horse, for she had never been afraid of it for a moment, but in herself—and when she had finished the treatment she allowed herself the vanity of muttering, "I bet even Dad couldn't have done it better. *Much* better, anyway."

She was getting colder by the minute, waist-deep in the muddy river. She touched the horse and whispered a good-bye, turned and trudged away. She suspected that her heart was breaking.

Spire was standing in his Yard, smirking at her fatly. She paused as she passed him and said, her voice choked, "What is that p-poor animal doing in the river?"

"She got a swole knee. Running water's good for it."

"Do you ever feed it?"

"Why, sure I feed her. I feed all my livestock good," he said, offended.

She went on to the car, thinking fiercely. Her father was putting something into the trunk. She got in, first spreading the old plaid car-robe over the seat, then folding its warm comforting thickness around her drenched body. Rand got in beside her and started the engine, clicked on the heater. "We'll have you home in a jiffy," he said.

"Forty miles of jiffy. I'm okay."

"You don't want a summer cold that'll hang on for weeks."

"Germs give you colds, not a little water."

He eyed her sideways. "If that's a little water, the Atlantic's a medium-sized puddle, miss."

"I'll be all right, honest. Promise."

"You know what I bought for eight dollars?" he asked, turning carefully and heading for the main road. "A Seth Thomas shelf clock. The real thing. It's in bad shape but in a week—"

"I don't even know whether it's a colt or a filly," said Julie miserably.

"Filly. In a week I can have it in first-class shape," he said. "The clock, not the horse, that is. You know how rare it is to find a Seth Thomas shelf clock? About as rare—"

"That man said she had a swollen knee. That could mean anything," said Julie bitterly. "And in that cold river she'll get flu. Or pneumonia. She'll die! She'll fall down and drown!"

"There, now, honey, try not to worry too much."

"How much is too much?" growled Julie, sunk in her despair. She thought for a mile or two, as Rand pushed the car to the speed limit and held it there. Then she said, hesitant, "How did you know I was at the river?"

"Why, I heard you yowling," he told her, smiling. "I thought you were being savaged by a wild chicken, and came running." He shook his head in mock wonder. "Just in time to see you dive into the current on your impetuous way to a horse."

"Dad, it isn't anything to joke about."

"I'm still a little shaken up, Julie, that's all."

"Oh. I'm sorry. But I couldn't leave it to k-kill itself with that chain!" She remembered, and looked down at her hands, which were smeared with rust and

blood where she'd wrestled with the chain. She dug
out her wet handkerchief, cleaned them, and rubbed
on some Furacin. "You just let me do it," she said.
"You didn't come to help. That . . . that isn't like
you, Dad."

"You were doing fine all by yourself, dear girl," he
said quietly. "I didn't want to butt in."

She realized that it was a high compliment. Then
she identified the strange expression he had worn. "And
you were actually proud of me," she said. "When I
was being so crazy."

"Not crazy, not in the sense my elderly generation
uses the word. Good and kind and—concerned. All
of them fine things to be, Julie. And brave, too: not
everyone would bounce into a cold, muddy river to help
an animal that might have been dangerous."

"She only stepped on my foot once," said Julie,
trying to grin. "You know, Dad, when you made me
put the medication on her by myself, I thought you
were mad at me." She writhed as a sudden streamlet
of icy water shot down her spine from her hair. "You're
so good with animals—"

"So are you. It was time you found that out." He
used the windshield wipers briefly to clear off a vast
splash of brown liquid thrown up by a passing
truck. "I'm not sure I can say this right, Julie, but I'll
try. I was shaken up when I saw how great you were
with that poor thing. I guess I recognized what's been
staring me in the face for a while."

"What?" she asked when he was silent.

"I still have a little girl for a daughter, thank the
powers," he said, "but I also have, in that same wet,
shivering skin, a very respectable beginning of a re-
sponsible adult. And that's quite a fact to discover in
a muddy dump like Spire's Original Swamp."

"Well," she said, "gee," she said, "thanks. Gosh,"
she added, after thinking it over, "thanks, Dad."

"My pleasure, Miss Jefferson."

They were wordless, perhaps a little embarrassed,
for a couple of miles. The heat began to dry Julie's

jeans and sweater, if not her long, saturated hair.

"You know," she said finally, "she has little bright flashes of mahogany in that poor dulled-up coat."

"Imagine that."

"She has good blood, I bet."

"Undernourished, I'm afraid, but perhaps basically good."

"But she'll *die* in that dreary place!"

"Oh, I hope not." He was being almost off-hand about it. She sensed something behind the bland smile.

"Dad," she said in a rush, "I have a hundred and two dollars and eighty cents in my bank account—"

He snapped his fingers abruptly. "I'll be dog-boned," he said. "I'll be everlastingly dog-boned and cats'-meated. I *knew* I'd forgotten to ask you something! Must have been that clock that put it out of my head."

"Ask me what?"

"How does it feel to be the owner of a real live horse? I bought that filly from Spire—and she's yours."

Chapter 3

It was a little after four when they reached home. Julie, still stricken with awe and gratitude, and boiling with plans that trod on one another's heels too fast to be properly analyzed, ran herself a hot bath and put on fresh jeans and blouse.

She rubbed her hair into a state resembling dryness, iodined the cuts on her hands, and went to sit at the kitchen table and face her father, who was drinking a cup of coffee. "How do we get her?" she asked him. "Where'll we keep her? Who—"

"One question to the second, please. We'll borrow a horse trailer somewhere."

"St. Clair's."

"Yes. Where else, indeed? Where will we keep her. Hmm. She'll need better pasturage than we can give her here, that's sure."

"Oh, Dad, I feel certain that if I—" she began with a rush.

"Whoa! Honey, you're strung up as tight as a fiddle string in Nashville."

"I know. I never owned a horse before. And I'm so worried about her in that river. And there are so many problems."

"We'll solve 'em one at a time. Here, have some hot milk," he said, going to the stove and pouring her a mugful.

"I don't want to go to *sleep!*"

36

"I anticipate that you'll go to sleep next Tuesday. Drink your milk. It prevents colds and fiddle-string snapping." He sat down again; the raccoon appeared from somewhere and clambered deliberately into his lap. "Hello, Burglar. Now. That filly's in bad shape. We don't know how serious the knee is, but she must have been starved for months. She's young, too."

"What's that got to do with it?"

Rand said patiently, "You know, if you pause to think, miss, that young horses are hit hardest by illness and malnutrition."

"Yes, I know," said Julie, ashamed. "Okay, I'll try to use my head."

"Luckily, she's got most of her growth. She's a pretty big horse—she's no yearling, but I wouldn't guess her to be much more than two. However, she is young and easily damaged. She needs more expert attention than we can give her, until she's cured of everything. I hope *everything* isn't as bad as—"

"As you believe it is."

"Yes. No sense in troublin' trouble till trouble troubles us, though. She may just be underfed and have a simple bump on the knee. The chain damage looked superficial to me."

"Some of it isn't good, Dad."

"Well, anyway, she needs real professional help."

"Stash!"

Rand frowned at the raccoon thoughtfully. Then he looked up. "Stash has his hands full with the St. Clair stable, Julie. I know he's your friend, but you can only ask so much by way of friendship."

"I'll help out with chores and horses and—oh, Dad, I do help Stash already, and he says I'm *truly* helpful, too, and he wouldn't know what to do without me on Sundays, and I can work harder, and besides he'll *want* to fix the filly up because he loves horses and if he'd seen her at Spire's he'd have bought her himself, if he'd had the money! Hey," she said, blinking, "I never thanked you for her! You can't afford to buy me horses, Dad. Was she an awful lot?"

"No. When I advertise that eight-dollar clock in the collectors' magazine, I'll make back her price and more."

"Oh, super. Is it that good?"

"A Seth Thomas shelf clock, signed on the dial and back plate? It's fantastic."

"I'm so glad," she said gratefully. "How am I ever going to thank you enough?"

"Just say Hi to me now and then as you pause here between visits to your filly," he chuckled. "All right, when you go over to beg the loan of a horse trailer, and I suppose you'll have to talk to Will Everett about that, you can discuss the veterinary aspects with Stash." He scratched the raccoon, Burglar, behind one ear. The little beast switched its bushy ringed tail with pleasure. "I don't imagine you were looking at that horse, Julie, with the eye of a future owner; you were too busy rescuing her. But she's a mighty nice looking girl. I wonder how in the world she landed at Spire's Original Cesspool?"

Julie gulped the last of the warm milk. "I can't imagine. She's so gentle, and she'd be pretty if she had some meat on her poor bones. Dad, can I go talk to Stash now?"

"If he's not too busy. Supper about six?"

"I'll be back by then. Dad?"

"Hmm?"

"Thanks a bunch. A large, flowery bunch with a balloon tied to it."

"If I'm bridging the generation gap correctly, that's a lot of thanks."

"I mean it, too," said Julie, and vanished from the kitchen as though she'd just heard her very own filly nicker outside the door. Rand picked Burglar up and laughed into the impassive little masked face. Burglar sniffed. He was not enthusiastic about horses.

Julie parked Bearcat on the gravel drive and walked up to the stable, which housed the St. Clair string of Thoroughbreds. She went along the row of stalls until she found Stash examining the shoes of a white-legged chestnut colt.

"Don't just like the way he's settin' down his feet," he said to Julie, emerging into the aisle. "And he's a mite cranky. You never can tell." He shook his head, deep in thought. He was a tall man, about the age and build of Rand Jefferson, with a skin like black silk except where it had been callused hard as bone in more than a qaurter-century of service to the St. Clairs. He was the head groom. If anyone in Ohio thought more of horses than Julie did, it must have been Stash Watkins. "We'll see, come morning," he said. 'You and me, we'll look him over good in the sun. We'll find what's frettin' him." He gave her a flick of his eyes. "You're a girl with somethin' on her mind," he said mildly.

"I have a horse," said Julie.

"Every girl should have a horse," said Stash reasonably. "Where you got him? In your hip pocket?"

"He—I mean she—she's at Spire's Yard near Amityville, and she's sick and hurt, and . . ."

The whole story poured out, sort of backward and upside-down, it seemed to Julie, but she got it told and hesitated, and Stash said, "First thing we have to do is bring her *here*," as if it were the most natural conclusion anyone would come to.

"Oh, I was going to ask you if—"

"First thing we have to do before that first thing, though, we got to chat it over with Mr. Everett. He's the foreman and what the foreman says, goes. First thing before them first things, you got to blow your nose and dry your eyes."

"Oh, Stash, I'm so happy and worried sick and excited, I can't think straight!"

"Not every day that a girl gets herself a filly," said Stash. "Come on, Mr. Everett's eatin' an early supper on account of his company just came home starved to pieces."

"He's got company? We can't interrupt him, then,"

Julie said, as her urgency rose in her and broke into more tears.

"Oh, the company won't mind. The company'll be pleased to see you." He walked off toward Will Everett's quarters, Julie trailing behind uncertainly. Would Stash do the talking? Will Everett, a robust man who was always in a terrible hurry and had a manner so brisk that she always felt guilty if she took up enough of his time to say good morning, was hardly more than a stranger to her.

She blew her nose. No, she'd do the talking. She had been complimented today on her responsibility and bravery. Earlier, she'd assured herself that she was now just about grown up. So she'd do the talking.

"Come in," said the rough, no-nonsense voice of the foreman to Stash's knock. They did. Julie yipped with surprise, riveted in her tracks.

"Monty!"

"Julie Jefferson?" The young man stood up, a head and a half taller than Julie, broader and leaner than she remembered, and looking very handsome, even though his civilian clothes were now such a poor fit that he looked as if he'd put them on for a joke. "It is Julie!" he said, taking her hands in his. "Man, have you changed for the better!"

"You too," said Julie, laughing. "Is two years gone already?"

"Yes, and one year and eleven months since I had the last letter from you," he said. He had just finished his hitch in the army.

"I'm a terrible correspondent, I know," she admitted.

"I carried your letter with me always," he said, so straightfaced that for a moment she thought he was serious. "It saved my life once. I was struck by a grenade fragment, but when they opened my shirt, the steel had embedded itself in your letter, saving me from harm. Wonderful what one page of paper can do."

"How come you never even answered it, after all that?"

"I didn't?" He was actually astonished. "Honest, I thought I had. I guess I'm as careless about old friendships as you are."

"Steak's getting cold," said Will Everett briefly. He jerked a finger at his son to sit down again. "Julie, you want a slab of beef? There's plenty."

"Oh, no thank you, Mr. Everett." She was delighted to see Monty after so long, but her filly was standing in a cold river forty miles to the south. "I . . . I have a big favor to ask you."

"Shoot," said Will Everett curtly.

He heard her out with far more patience than she had expected, eating and glancing up now and then under tickets of eyebrows. Monty ate too, watching her affectionately. They had been friends almost all Julie's life, even though he was four years older than she; and at one time, when she was about fourteen, she had fancied for a whole month that she was in love with him. She remembered that, suddenly, and got her speech confused and stumbled around in words for a horrible minute. But Everett just kept eating and said nothing.

After telling him about the filly's condition and the circumstances in which they'd found her, she stated as emotionlessly as possible that if she could borrow a stall and Stash's skill, she would gladly pay him back with all the work she could do. Sundays and evenings. For as long as he wanted.

He laid down his knife and fork. She had a premonition that he was going to say, "All right, twenty years of work ought to pay for it," or something equally appalling. But he only looked at Stash and said, "This sounds like your idea."

"No," said Julie, just as Stash said, "Yep."

"Always knew you two would gang up on me someday," said Everett. "I'm not crazy about keeping somebody's horse, with what kind of germs and diseases heaven knows, and having my head groom fussing over it night and day. I tell you that plain, Julie, I'm not crazy about the idea."

"Dad," Monty said, "I can help with the filly, too. And Julie always was a lot of help around here."

"You? You're going to learn to be a racing trainer. That's a full-time job."

"So was the army a full-time job, but I did have half-hours now and then to do other things. Everybody can't work at their job every waking minute like you do," said Monty quietly.

"Well, they ought to. But I guess I can't reform the world. Okay. I don't like it, but you're a nice kid, Julie, and you do make yourself useful, Stash tells me. And your father's as fine a man as walks the earth," he added brusquely, astounding her.

I guess I always thought nobody else really appreciated Dad, she thought. Then it dawned on her that Everett had agreed to take in her horse. She stuttered her thanks. "It's only till she's cured, of course."

"What? Where'll you keep her then?" he barked.

"Why, why, I don't know . . ."

"If she gets better, she'll live here. No better place for her. Can't picket her out on your lawn, for Pete's sake." He started to eat again. "You understand, Julie," he said, more slowly and kindly than she'd ever heard him speak, "if the filly's too bad, we'll have to put her down."

"I know. But I don't believe she is."

"We'll see. Stash, get her one of the horse trailers, will you?"

"Right away, Mr. Everett," said Stash happily.

"Wait a minute," Monty said, "Julie, you going for her now? I'll drive you. We can use a car that's rigged to take a trailer."

"You haven't finished your steak," said Will.

"Dad, that's my *third*. I'm up to here with food. Best I've had in two years, but I can't manage another bite."

"Then go ahead." He shook his head at them. "I must have bog spavin of the brains, bringing a sick cart horse onto a Thoroughbred breeding farm. Time

I thought about retiring," said this abrupt, vigorous, unpredictable man.

"Mr. Everett," said Julie impulsively, as she followed Stash and Monty through the door, "you're very sweet." As they walked down the hall, she heard him burst out with one muffled, amazed word.

"Sweet!"

Monty chuckled all the way to the trailer.

Chapter 4

"It's about a mile farther, on the left," said Julie. "You'll see the sign. It's something to see, too."

"Fine. Did I tell you how glad I am to see *you* again, Julie?"

"And I'm really glad you're home safe, Monty," she said, a little ashamed that she hadn't said that before; they'd been talking horses all the way, except for the time when Julie remembered that she was due home at six, and they'd had to find a phone and call her father. "Was it bad?"

"Not too. It went fast. I missed the horses, but there was plenty to keep me occupied."

"Was there truly shrapnel flying around? Never mind the funny stuff about my letter, either."

"I wasn't even out of the *States*."

"Oh. I guess I did lose touch, didn't I?"

"Sure did. There's your sign."

"Brace yourself. The Yard's a blot on the landscape."

They drove in the side road and stopped. Monty whistled. "You weren't kidding." They got out and hurried toward the river, avoiding the scrap metal and apathetic chickens. Spire emerged from his house and intercepted them.

"Hey, you're the kid owns the horse."

"Yes. We came for her."

"Wasn't expectin' you till tomorrow. I got maybe bad news for you." Julie's heart went into a power dive and she felt sick. Spire's gummy voice went on. "She fell down in the river. You went and shortened that chain, and she fell down."

"That doesn't make any sense at all," said Julie. "What would a shorter chain have to do with it?"

"I dunno, but she hadn't fell down before," said Spire. "She put a gash into that swole knee. She's up now, Mind, but she's favorin' that leg and—"

"Let's see her," said Monty, urgent. They dashed on, Spire wallowing in their wake like a fat, dirty little tugboat pursuing a pair of racing sloops.

The filly stood in the shallows of the river; the current was faster and the water lapped at her legs just above the knees. Julie was about to plunge in, without a thought of a second soaking, but Spire yelled, "Don't do that! I'll bring her in." Leaning out from the big oak, he caught the chain with an old piece of iron like a shepherd's crook and jerked it hard.

"Don't knock her down!" cried Julie, in agony. "She's so weak . . ."

"I won't." As the chain came tight, Spire, with surprising carefulness, drew it in, and the filly, throwing her head up with short sluggish gestures of protest, followed the pull on her halter until she stood on the mud of the bank.

Monty whistled. "Julie, she's not in good shape."

"But she'll get well," said Julie firmly, trying to believe it. She went to the horse, which seemed too tired and ill to recognize her. "Can you take the chain off this halter?" she asked Spire.

He extracted a pair of long-nose pliers from his hip pocket and cut the wire that fastened rusty iron to rotting leather. "You know, I explained to your pop, the halter don't go with her," he said.

Julie stared at him. "I don't want your halter!"

"It's an antique," said Spire, half apologetic.

"I can see that," she said, choking with anger; as if she would have left this piece of miserable slimy stuff on her beautiful horse! "You can have it as soon as she's in the trailer."

Taking the old leather in her right hand, she began to walk the filly up the bank. Slowly they crested the rise and traversed the rats' nest of the Yard. The horse limped beside her, head now drooping dully. Julie, distraught, wondering whether the bone had been chipped in this latest misfortune of the poor beast, scarcely heard Monty talking to her. They came to the trailer. Monty let down the tailgate and, taking the horse from Julie, walked it up into the interior.

She did not balk; either she was used to horse trailers, or she was too far gone to care where they put her.

Monty took the halter off her neck and tossed it out to Spire, who was shuffling his feet in the background. Then the young man gently slipped a decent traveling headstall on her and snapped two chains onto its rings. He had decided to leave the partition in place, dividing the trailer in half, so that she would have less room to move about in. The chains were attached to the center post and the side of the trailer, preventing the filly from turning around in the single stall, which would have been very bad. She now stood, dripping and still, in as safe a traveling box as she could have had: before her was the wooden, leather-padded breast bar; along both sides were thick layers of foam rubber, covered with leather; under her hoofs was a heavy rubber mat. Monty had opened the louvered shutters of the little window in front of her, so that light came in to cheer her—if that was possible.

He put up the tailgate and closed her in.

"Well, good luck," said Spire. "You got a real bargain in that there horse. Make a good riding horse for you."

"Has she eaten today?" Julie asked.

"I feed my livestock good. She had some hay. Didn't eat it all, there was so much."

"Good-bye," said Julie, getting into the car without looking at him. She could imagine the state that hay must have been in.

Monty drove home with all possible caution. He did not say much, recognizing the fact that Julie was too apprehensive about the filly to enjoy any conversation just then. They came to the St. Clair Farm in early twilight, and stopped before the stable.

The horse was leaning heavily against the side of the trailer, her feet propped against the base of the partition. Hardly the proper stance for shipping in a trailer but the chance that she had hurt herself any further was slight, with all the softness around her. Stash materialized out of nowhere, eased in beside her and steadied her on her feet. He unsnapped the chains and backed her gently out.

"My," he said in a mild tone, "she does need a touch of lookin' after, don't she?" He led her off to a vacant stall and as she stood waiting with infinite, sad patience, not looking at any of them, the groom hustled into action. "Gonna need both of you to help, so don't wander off," said he, and vanished, to return within a minute with both arms laden.

"First she gets a tetanus shot, to keep off the lock-jaw. Mr. Monty, you stand by her head, 'case she don't take kindly to the needle." He was so expert that she never moved. "That's a grand girl," said Stash approvingly. "Well now, that off fore knee is the worst, I'd guess. Bad swellin', nasty cut, some fever in it. Hand me them antibiotical medicaments, Julie, if you please." In what seemed a very brief time even to Julie, who was afire with worry, he had treated and bandaged the knee. "Bucket of crushed ice," said Stash crisply, like an intense doctor to a nurse in a television play, to Monty, who disappeared in his turn.

Antibiotics and sterile bandages were placed swiftly and professionally on all the open wounds from nose to croup, after thorough cleansing. As the filly grew more and more patched with neat white squares and oblongs, Julie realized that she had been even more hurt by the chain than she'd noticed. Above the point of her shoulder, from stem to stern she was as much white now as bay.

Stash talked constantly, soothing both horse and girl. "Tomorrow first thing, you kite down to the swamp and get you some lilies."

"Lilies?" Julie repeated blankly.

"You know, cabbage. Skunk cabbage. We always call 'em lilies. With them big leaves, you know?"

"Oh, sure."

"You bring me up a whole mess of lily leaves and I wrap 'em around the legs here, you see, and the lily leaves they make their own water, and draw out the flames from the poor legs, and they help a lot more'n some of these modern medicaments, Julie."

"Okay, as soon as it's light enough to see. Stash, what caused the swelling on that knee? She had it before she fell down today and gashed it."

"Oh, now," he said, making the filly lift one leg and dexterously tugging on a long, loose rubber boot, into which he carefully poured some of the crushed ice that Monty had brought. "Takes the fire out. Now, Julie, you *know* nobody can say where that swell came from. Any old knock or fall." He put on another of the boots. The filly had turned her head and was watching him with some of the light of interest that Julie had seen in her eyes at their first meeting. "She may not be so bad off in that knee as she looks, and then, she may be worse. Can't tell this early. But don't lose sleep over it, 'cause that *never* helps a thing in this world; and besides, she got a look to her face right now says, I'm a far piece from the end of the line."

"You see that too," said Julie, grateful.

"Hard to miss it when you keep one eye open," said Stash. "She ain't had a half-square meal for a long whiles, though. Think you remember how to fix up a hot bran mash?" he asked Monty. "After all them years away from civilization? I can do it if you forgot, but I still got vet-work to do here."

"I remember," said Monty, and left once more.

"This is so good of you, Stash," said Julie.

"Ah, shoo," he grinned, and continued with his

remedies and examinations. Finally he said, straightening up, "You have a fine big filly here, Julie, if she comes round."

Julie stared at the horse. She had not realized until now that it was big for a two-year-old female: sixteen hands or a little more. "She's going to be pretty, isn't she, Stash?"

"Indeed. Look at that topline, that's as pretty as they make 'em. Has a good crest to her neck. Good muscles, blame tired but tough, you know? Good lines all over. Put a lot o' meat onto her and she'll be as pretty for a horse as you are for a girl."

"Gee," said Julie, struck almost dumb by the double compliment.

When the hot bran mash was ready for her, they held their breath, all three of them. Would she eat it?

She would.

"Oh wow," said Julie thankfully.

"Now," said Stash, "you go home to supper, and get a rest, and I'll see you with them lily leaves about six or so, right? And we'll all think good thoughts, and if everything works out, well, it'll all work out. That's the first thing we all gotta do for the month or two comin' up—think good thoughts about this fine hungry girl."

So Julie took a last long look at her own horse, and went home to supper.

All night long, between the intervals of sleep, she did as Stash had ordered, and thought good thoughts about the wasted, fragile, wounded, lovely animal that her father had given her for a growing-up present.

From the collecting of big skunk cabbage leaves at earliest dawn, through an endless string of chores on the breeding farm, to the last visit with her filly at sundown, Julie never seemed to stop moving. She was so eager to learn everything about the job of stable-girl that Stash felt obliged to slow her down once or twice.

"Can't take over my *whole* job, Julie, else I'll be lookin' for work."

She glanced up from currying the chestnut colt. "I'm not tired, honest, Stash; and you know I love this!"

"Be lovin' it from a bed o' pain tomorrow," he said darkly. "You're creatin' the sorest set of muscles this side of a coal mine. Slack off."

"Will you teach me to fix that tonic for the big gray, Dovewing? I know it's iron and liver extract and—"

"Please," said Stash, grinning in spite of himself, "don't try to do more'n six things at a time. One Mr. Everett to a stable is plenty."

And he'd been right, of course: she went to bed that night so tired she hurt, and woke up stiffer than wrought iron.

When she hobbled in at dawn to visit with her filly, Stash was already there with her, examining the bad knee. "I don't like it much at all," he said in answer to her breathless question. "Looks worse than when she came here." He always told her the truth, fearing to raise her hopes. For days his answer to her inevitable first query varied only from "Poorly," to "Pretty seedy." The filly showed no improvement until the next Friday, when at last Stash said cautiously, "Well, maybe a *mite* perked up," and Julie did a cartwheel in the stable aisle.

And that evening they named her. The three of them were visiting in her stall and for the first time she was plainly aware of them, as individual beings, as people who were trying to cure her illness. She nudged each of them softly as they came within her reach, and the big gentle eyes were brighter.

"She's a bonnie lass," said Monty, "she'll make it."

"That's it," exclaimed Julie. "I've been trying to decide on a name for her, and that's it—Bonnie."

"Good name," said Stash.

"*Your* name," said Julie gravely to the horse. "You're Bonnie."

Bonnie whiffled lightly.

"She says okay, that'll do her fine." Stash moved away. "Now we leave her get a night's sleep. She got a long way to go 'fore she's out of the briar patch."

Slowly, so slowly, she did begin to pick up, to look less like a hide-rack and to move like a horse instead of a marionette with broken strings. The fine neck arched proudly now and then as she welcomed Julie, and the bay coat, free now of all but two small bandages, showed its mahogany highlights quite plain. She favored her right foreleg, the one that had been hurt; but less, thought Julie, than before.

"I think she'll survive," said Monty at the end of two weeks.

"Certainly she'll survive!"

"I don't feel so bad about leaving tomorrow, then."

"Leaving?"

"I'm going out on the racing circuit with St. Clair's string. Be gone till September or later."

"But that's more than two months," protested Julie.

He teased her. "Will you really miss me that much?"

"No. But Bonnie will. Nobody will ever make her as good a stablemate as you." Julie gazed up at him innocently; she knew as well as anyone that horses' stablemates ranged from barnyard hens through goats to Shetland ponies, but seldom if ever included young men.

Monty chuckled. "You sub for me while I'm gone, Julie. Just bray like a donkey occasionally, and Bonnie will never know the difference."

And the next day he left, in the first of two big horse vans, with the runners.

Julie did miss him. She had grown to like Monty very much in those two weeks as they fussed together over Bonnie's curing; she thought, I don't know him as well as I did before he went to the army, but that's because he's a much more complex person now. I'm not always sure what he's thinking. But I know it's good.

She went to talk it over with Bonnie.

Chapter 5

If anyone had reminded Julie that she had been looking forward (only a few weeks ago!) to a summer of monotony and boredom, it would have made her eyes pop. Already, it seemed, she had become a career woman, with two jobs that took up every waking minute and made her life a kind of wonderful fantasy. It was exhilarating, exhausting, a quite incredible dream turned into reality.

Not that the business of clerking in the antique and gift shop took on any fresh fascination; that remained a plain job, to be done because it earned her keep and gave Dad the time to repair, renovate, and restore antiques. But now she could spend almost all her time there in thinking about her horse, while performing her tasks as efficiently (and mechanically) as ever. Building stables in the air, Rand Jefferson dubbed it; he knew how happy it made her, and he was content.

The dogs, Cissy and Joey, missed her badly, for she was up before the sun every day and off to St. Clair's, sometimes home for dinner but often not, and at the stable again until bedtime.

Her morning visits with Bonnie were all too brief, for she was scrupulous about arriving at the store by eight thirty. The evenings and Sundays were better, for then she could care for Bonnie, help her recuperate with vitamins, grooming, medicines, and companion-ship. She could also work for Stash, who was so pleased with her intelligence and developing skills that he had promoted her from cleaning and feeding chores to more complex and difficult work with the horses themselves, even veterinary tasks.

Every day Julie would recognize distinct signs of the filly's physical improvement, as though during the nights a wizard dropped by and did a little magic for her. But then, as Stash told her, "With a horse as bad off as she was, Julie, there ain't a way in the world to get but better. And one that low and poorly, if she doesn't hustle up and get there fast, she won't get there at *all*." It was only then that Julie allowed herself to realize, with a shudder, how close to death Bonnie had really been.

Stash was not usually available in the evenings, so that Julie had to deal with the filly's work and training pretty much on her own; it was a considerable chal-lenge. Training . . . yes, the time had come, she told herself one hot July night, as she watched Bonnie walking her stall. A bad nervous habit in an older animal, it seemed with Bonnie only an indication of a newly found feeling of freshness and energy, brought on by large doses of vitamins and food and idleness. Tomorrow, Saturday, she'd talk to Stash about it. She had no idea whether the filly had even been broken to bridle and saddle.

So the next afternoon she led her horse from the stall, fully tacked in saddle, bridle and martingale—by Stash, at his insistence. "You don't know how wicked these young uns can be 'fore they been broke. She loves you, all right, but she's skittish and high-stringed, and she could crowd you slam against that partition without ever meanin' to do you no harm at all," he'd said. Bonnie had indeed given him some back-talk before he'd bridled her, but she was only spirited, Julie was sure of it. Not mean. Not her filly.

They walked her down to the exercise track. She was excited, staring around her with eyes widened, almost swaggering as she inhaled the grass-scent and felt the sun hot on her hide.

"Now you act as if you're coolin' her out, hear me?" said Stash firmly. "I don't want to see one o' your feet in a stirrup. I got about half an hour's stuff to get done; you just tramp round an' round with her, no matter what she says or what you want to do."

"But she obviously knows about being ridden! She took the girth being tightened without a murmur!"

"Remember you work for me," said Stash. "Do like I tell you. Be back 'fore you can fidget twice."

They marched around the track, Bonnie now and then straining to pull out of Julie's grip. After about three months, according to the girl's reckoning, Stash reappeared.

"Right. Now I'll give you a leg up but you gotta be quick 'cause I'm gonna keep a holt of her in case she gets cute. Okay? Sure it is," he answered himself, "seen you do it often enough. Ready?"

"Ready."

She was in the saddle.

She was actually in the saddle atop her own two-year-old *horse*.

It was very hard to believe it.

Stash led her out. Bonnie wanted to get away from him, that was plain. Stash refused to release her. They did two circles of the track.

"Plenty for today."

"Oh, but she's been in that stall so long and —"

"And you want to let her breeze. Get down now, Julie. You got to go about this the right way and hold your wantin' in hard. If we knew somethin' about her before you fished her out o' that crick, we could go faster. But we don't, and we can't. 'Sides, she's still favorin' that leg that got cut. She's had enough for today."

Julie dismounted obediently. Stash was always right. They took her back and she drank some water thirstily and thrust her wet nose against Julie's cheek. It was plainly a sign of great affection.

"Somebody's treated her well, back before *it* hap-pened to her," Julie said.

"Yep. Maybe tomorrow you can walk her 'thout me at the head. Maybe not. We'll see."

Stash was cautious, but gradually they both came to realize that Bonnie, although possessing a natural spirit, was also an intelligent mount and had no desire to throw her rider. In a week the limp was quite gone, and Julie was saddling and bridling her alone, and trotting briskly around the exercise track, no Stash in sight.

July passed, and August. They grew to know each other, truly to become part of each other as they trotted and cantered and occasionally galloped together. Stash had forbidden any serious track-style galloping until Monty's return. "You ain't never galloped a horse in your life, Julie, and you need trainin' just like a horse needs it; only more so, 'cause you're in charge when you're up. You can wait."

"I can wait," said Julie, hoping it was true, and that she wouldn't burst like a roman candle before someone instructed her. Secretly she believed that she could gallop Bonnie for miles . . .

Bit by bit Stash fed her horse-wisdom, lore that he'd collected all his life, and in spite of the fact that Bonnie sometimes taxed her skill and strength to the limit, she was able to control the horse completely. Stash, watching them romp around the meadow together like a pair of fillies, shook his head thoughtfully. "Some horse," he said aloud to himself. "Some mighty lot o' horse. Where'd you come from, anyway, horse, to end up rollin' beside that little girl in that sweet grass? I give a lot to know. A *lot*."

In September Monty came back, burned dark and worked leaner than ever, bringing a couple of St. Clair's top stakes winners home for a rest from the racing circuit. As soon as his father had fed him a large steak, he went out riding with Julie.

He was deeply impressed. He had not seen her ride since she was fifteen; she had a way with the big powerful filly, a genuine rider's way. She was bright and strong, willing and quick to learn.

He could use someone like that to help him break the yearlings.

Saying nothing about this to her, he observed the fashion in which she worked with various horses: saw how competently she handled Dovewing, the gray stallion who suffered from a blood deficiency and occasionally needed a tonic, which she prepared and administered—and Dovewing wouldn't allow just *any-one* near him; how she could spot potential leg troubles, the bane of Thoroughbred breeders, nearly as quickly as Stash himself could. And of course she rode only Bonnie, but her skill was improving, her courage unquestionable. She had excellent hands and sat her horse well.

Julie was a born horsewoman. Too good to lose. Besides, they were friends.

"Julie," he said one day, as they headed for the stable, "how'd you like a job?"

"I have two," she smiled. "One for my father and one for yours."

"Stash tells Dad that you've made yourself so useful, St. Clair is making Bonnie's keep *plus* a profit."

"I'm glad. That's how it ought to be. It's a lifesaver, being able to keep her here." Julie glanced over at him. "What did you mean, a job?"

"A real job. Helping me break the yearlings, maybe some other training duties. Full-time."

Julie stared at him. At last she said, voice hushed, "Oh, that would be plain out of sight! Do you think I could?"

"Do you?"

"Yes," she said steadily.

"Then I'll talk to Dad about it."

"Look, Monty, I'd love to do it for you free . . . You know, I enjoy just being here with the horses so much— but if I didn't work at the store, Dad would have to hire someone else to clerk and clean, so I'd have to make enough to let him do that. I'm sorry."

"I never meant to acquire your services for nothing, miss," he said, laughing. "I'm a grasping old skinflint, sure, but not *that* bad. If my father okays the plan, I'll take you on for a couple of months at your replacement's wages plus your expenses; and if you work out, as I think you will," he leaned over and poked her in the ribs with one finger, "why then, Bob Cratchit, I will raise your salary!"

"Mr. Scrooge," said Julie a little shakily, "I don't know what to say."

"Try 'oh, super.' "

"That's sort of inadequate." They dismounted at the stable. She shook hands with him solemnly. "Wait here," she said, giving him Bonnie's reins. She ran as fast as she could until she was far enough from the horses not to startle them. Then she threw back her head and let out a shrill, loud whoop of happiness. After which she returned sedately to Monty's side. "If I'd held that in until I got home," she said, "I'd have gotten hysterical."

"Working with you is going to be quite an experience," he told her, "I can see that now. Well, it's settled, then, if Dad goes for the idea. There's no guarantee that he will."

"He just has to," said Julie with fervor.

After their meal that night, she said to Rand Jefferson, "I have something to tell you, or ask you, or both, I mean," and her father leaned back and eyed her and said, "I know all about it," and Julie said, astonished, "Did Monty—" and her father nodded. "We had a long talk this morning."

"And it's all right?"

"If Will Everett agrees. It's fine with me. The sort of thing you were born for, I guess. If you were any other teen-age girl I'm acquainted with, I'd put my foot down so hard it'd go through the floor. But you can handle it, and it will make you happy, and that's all that's important to me."

"You are the perfect father."

"Only because I have a perfect daughter."

"Yes, but I *mean* it, Dad."

"I know, honey. So do I."

"Aren't we lucky?" she breathed.

"So lucky we have to work very hard to deserve such luck."

"Even if Mr. Everett says no, I'm the most fortunate girl in Ohio!"

At about the same moment, Will Everett was feeling decidedly put-upon. His son had been bombarding him with quotations from Stash, snowing him with facts about Julie Jefferson and her abilities (perhaps a little exaggerated), and in short, giving him no peace. He gazed at his son with a scowl.

"Why is it that even when only one of you's here, I always get to feeling that I'm surrounded? That girl is more trouble than she's—no," he said, being a fair man, if abrupt, "she's been worth her salt, I give her that. But you and she and that blame groom have a habit of hemming me in and making me say yes when good sense tells me I should be saying no."

"This is my idea, Dad, and it's a good one. Stash approves."

"I was *sure* of that," said the older man glumly.

"She'll be better than any boy we could hire—"

"Prettier, you mean."

"I don't want to hire her because she's a girl, or because she's pretty, but because she's good and getting better every day. She'll be a real investment. The way she handles that filly—"

"You're repeating yourself. You gave me the facts. It's against my better judgment. But," said Will Everett, scowling even blacker, "if she wants to break her fool neck on those yearlings, I'll give her a chance. But let me catch the two of you galloping off into the sun-rise on our good stakes horses, and back she goes to her dolls and tea parties. Got that?"

"Of course, Dad. Don't forget, I'm a trainer, I —"

"You're learning to be one. Don't get stuck on yourself yet. Remember, she's not to handle the good horses on the string. On that condition, I'll try her out."

"Right," said Monty, knowing better than to make a fuss about thanks and gratitude. "I'll hire her tomorrow on a trial basis."

"And one more thing. Aside from her neck being broken. If so much as one blond hair on her head's hurt, Montgomery Everett, the *both* of you can look for another job!"

Chapter 6

It took three days to locate a young lady in Blankton who would go to work in the Emporium; then Julie, having drilled her for a day in the simple duties and functions of the place, reported to Monty and her own new job.

"You have to learn all about breaking them," Monty told her, "and working them out, and conditioning—though you already know plenty about that—and, later on, schooling. Then there's . . ."

"I'm not sure I know what schooling is."

"That's racetrack shorthand for breaking out of the starting gate. Sometimes you have to keep schooling them all their racing lives; sometimes they catch on and that's that. Dovewing was barred from the track for two months, some years ago, because he'd get nasty at the gate. It took that long to get him okayed out of the gate so we could run him again. But that comes later. First, breaking."

So she began. Now of course, breaking a Thoroughbred need not be the rough and dangerous practice it sounds like. When it is gently done, with vast patience and much soothing friendliness, its ultimate result, achieved in six or eight weeks, is a mannerly yearling that is ridable under normal conditions and prepared to go into serious training early in its two-year-old year.

Julie took to it like a kitten to tuna. The yearlings

for the most part responded to her as Bonnie had, and the stable pony who was used extensively in the breaking work grew to adore her too. "No doubt about who'd win a popularity contest with the animals on this farm," said Monty with admiration one cool October afternoon. "You're doing fine, Julie. In fact, it's time now you learned the techniques of galloping, because one day soon you'll be needing them."

"I don't mind," said Julie carelessly. She had been dying to learn, ever since Bonnie had recovered.

"The racing string is off limits, but you can use Bonnie. She ought to be safe enough by this time; the two of you remind me of a centaur when you canter."

"I'll be glad to," said Julie, nonchalant.

"And that phony indifference isn't fooling me a bit."

"I didn't think it was."

"Saddle up, pardner."

"Shore thing, bossman." She dashed away, heart thumping with anticipation.

Monty was mounted on the stable's "work" horse, an exercise horse slower than the racers but fast enough to use in workouts, where its purpose was to incite the other horse to speed. Julie walked her filly up beside it.

"Jack up your irons, Jock," said Monty. She reached down and shortened her stirrups so that her heels were drawn up under her seat in a fair imitation of a race rider's pose.

"Hold on a minute," said Monty with a grin, "you'll never make it long enough to jog in that position. Your muscles will protest loudly for sure. Takes a while to get used to riding this short. Drop those at least three holes." Julie adjusted one. "That's about right." She matched the other to its length.

"Now make a C with your body."

"A sea?"

"Just stick your feet on the dashboard, leave your hands where they are and curve your body into a letter C. That's good.

"Now take a cross with your reins and put the bridge

on her neck. She shouldn't take much of a hold, but if she gets too strong just lean down on your hands. And remember, once you get set don't try to change your hold 'cause if she did want to get away from you that's all the chance she'd need. Not that I expect Bonnie to try it, but a racehorse will and it's no fun trying to rate one once he's got his head loose."

"Oh beans, I know that."

"Hush up and listen. Unwind. This filly probably won't pull a pound, but it's a good way for you to learn the game. Let's go."

They walked out, then jogged, and almost before she realized it they had moved into the faster speed.

I'm galloping, she told herself, and it was as fantastic to her as though she had said, I'm flying. And surely the sensations must be much alike, the wind of their own making tearing past them, the ground flowing along in a blur, nothing in the world but horse and girl and everything around them indistinct and unimportant. With an effort of will, Julie managed to remember not to let the filly out to her full potential, because she had no idea how fast that might be, or whether she could control her at top speed. Bonnie plainly yearned to go even faster; it became a real struggle to keep her to a kind of "under wraps" gait.

In the big body under her she fancied she could feel more power than she'd have dreamed possible in any animal. Certainly that great thrusting head and neck were almost more than she could hold in. It was like straddling a thunderbolt.

Maybe it's like this when you gallop. Maybe there's nothing phenomenal in it at all. I never went so fast before and . . . well, I won't talk about it to Monty, I might just make a fool of myself if I did. Every horse on the place must feel like a rocket when it runs in two's with the work horse.

She feels like Superhorse, though.

Long before she was ready to slow down, Monty signaled her to do so. Reluctantly she brought Bonnie, not without some difficulty, down to a walk. The filly turned her head back and blew through her soft lips loudly.

"Me too," said Julie. "It was lovely."

Monty came up beside them. "We'll try that again tomorrow morning. You did pretty well. How'd you like it?"

"It was really neat."

He frowned down at Bonnie. "Maybe you ought to drill on one of ours that I know. This beast is still a mystery in a lot of ways."

"Pooh," said Julie airily, "not to me."

"Ho ho ho, said the jolly green rider. You *were* holding her in fairly hard, weren't you?"

"Well, yes."

"She has a long stride even for a racer, from what I could see. I'll watch you from the ground when you've become used to galloping. But I'm sure her stride's longer than average. And if she were really let out—"

"What if?"

"Nothing. Never mind. I just wonder, that's all. I wonder my head off about that horse of yours."

"What exactly do you wonder?"

"What she did before she went to visit Spire, naturally. One thing she did, I'll tell you, and that's run. Plenty. Now we'll play hot-walkers for a while. And incidentally," he said, "congratulations, Julie."

"On what?"

"Galloping without falling off." She grinned. He said, "I am not joking, honest. You did well."

Julie was immensely pleased.

The lessons went well, though it was often hard to hold Bonnie in, and sometimes her arms would ache with the strain. They were running in luck with the weather, which was mild and dry for an Ohio October. And then it happened: one morning the work horse pulled up lame.

"It's probably nothing serious," said Monty, after checking the leg and examining the hoof carefully. "But this puts me in a fix. I have to work Tuxedo this morning." This was the St. Clair stable's top stakes winner. "I can't neglect her, I really have to run her. Oh, blast!"

"Use Bonnie to run with her."

"No, there has to be some other answer."

"Well, why? What's wrong with Bonnie?"

"Nothing, but . . . I'm talking without thinking," he said, blinking at the filly. "She'll do. You're ready for it, you can hold her to just about what we've been doing, can't you?"

"I haven't lost control of her yet, have I? Why should I get myself dumped just because she's running with another horse?"

"You're right. And I don't have any other choice, do I?"

"None whatever. We'll wait quietly here, smelling the autumn breeze, till you come back," said Julie, dismounting. As he led the lame horse toward the stable, she said to Bonnie in a conspirator's whisper, "I'll bet Tuxedo won't beat you by much, will she?"

Bonnie agreed with her by pawing the ground, saying clearly that Pegasus himself would only outrace her by using his wings.

"Immodest," said Julie, "but true."

Shortly Monty returned with the stable's top mare. She was a large chestnut with three white legs and a star. "Remember, Julie," said the young man, "she has to keep up with the champ here. Just try to keep them head and head for the first half. That should be long enough to press Tux into gear and then you can ease off Bonnie and let Tux do her thing. I'll breeze on another half and then ease up myself. And Julie?"

"Yes"

"Don't let Bonnie try too hard. Once Tux pulls away, just pat her or something."

"I know. I'll do my best to console her."

"Okay, wise apple, this is the plan. We'll jog three-eighths, pull up and turn back. Then break off at the mile pole, gallop a mile and breeze a mile. When we hit that pole the second time we ought to be really moving so start to move her up at the seven-eighths and keep at her till the half, and . . ."

"You fuss too much, Monty. Let's go."

The two fillies stepped lightly onto the track and immediately began a brisk trot. Sleek hides rippled over bulging muscles that swiftly stretched and leaped into action.

Julie kept an eye on the marker poles—sixteenth, eighth, sixteenth, three-eighths—and pulled up as planned. Both horses jigged excitedly as they turned back to the mile pole.

"Now don't forget to begin your move early," said Monty with a smile, "and then try to hang in with us to the half."

When they reached the big blue and white pole that marked a mile from start to finish, they once again reversed their horses and headed counterclockwise around the track, galloping smoothly.

As the half-mile pole loomed ahead Julie felt a sudden prickling of excitement. Bonnie was moving easily, but something felt different—as if she were slowly gathering together into a giant coiled spring. Just past the three-quarters Julie saw Monty seem to fold up slightly, crouching low on Tuxedo's neck. She followed his example and by the time they came to the last sixteenth Julie knew that this would be no ordinary ride.

Monty turned and looked at Julie. "All set?" he shouted through the wind and waving mane.

Julie nodded.

"Let's go!"

Julie felt her filly explode beneath her like a beautiful missile. Thereafter (it seemed to her, remembering afterward) she stopped thinking entirely and only felt, acting from instinct, as the great animal under her took over the management of everything.

The two horses met the mile mark as one—tails flying—necks outstretched—suddenly longer and leaner, their hoofs barely skimming the ground.

Paired with a horse that could really run, Bonnie

could not be restrained. They roared around the track matching stride for stride, Bonnie on the outside, Tuxedo fairly hugging the rail. The brightly painted poles flashed by in a blur of color—blue for the quarters, red for the eighths, black for the sixteenths. Somewhere along the back side, Bonnie eased into a seemingly effortless stride. "Ease" Julie thought later—a strange word for the tremendous drive and power pulsing beneath her, but it was all that fitted. One instant the filly was flying and the next she was rocketing and to Julie it all felt perfectly natural.

Suddenly the chestnut mare was losing ground, and as Bonnie began to draw ahead Julie was tempted to move in on the rail "just to see what it was like." Such a move was quickly dismissed from her mind as she realized she might inadvertently cut across Tuxedo's line.

"Don't know when Monty's going to make his move," she thought, "but I don't want to be in the middle of it and that's for sure."

Having decided to stay right where she was, Julie simply rode her horse, moving with her as a fluid whole, scorching around the track and leaving the pride of the St. Clair Farm absolutely nowhere.

Then Monty was waving and howling at her to pull up. Automatically she stood in her irons and pulled back on the reins. The filly obliged this request almost immediately and eased herself up in less than a furlong.

"Good grief! Now what've we done?" Julie muttered to Bonnie as they turned back to join Tuxedo and her gaping rider.

Now Julie addressed herself to Monty while trying desperately not to appear winded. "What's the matter?"

"Matter? That filly of yours outran Tux—that's what's the matter!"

"You mean she ran with her a mile?" Julie cried in disbelief.

"Not only *with* her, but *past* her," he paused to emphasize each word.

"Well, Tux slowed down——"

"Slowed down, bull! She was going great guns. But Bonnie beat her."

Julie smoothed the black mane with pride and disbelief. "Really?" Then it hit her, the full force of it. "*Bonnie* beat *Tuxedo*?"

"By a full sixteenth of a mile."

"Man," Julie breathed.

"You didn't even know?"

"Well, I wasn't thinking much. I knew we passed Tux but . . . Say, she didn't pass us back, did she? You beat her," she told Bonnie proudly.

"Oh, brother, did you," said Monty, sliding to the ground. He came to Bonnie's head. Forty or fifty thoughts fell all over one another in his mind, fighting for clarification and statement, but all he could think to do was lift the filly's upper lip and memorize her identification tattoo. Six, seven, three, nine, five, four.

He repeated it aloud. He knew he would never forget it. Any more than he would forget this day and this incredible work, when the top stakes winner of a fine breeding farm was beaten into the track by a two-year-old mysterious stranger out of a dirty little river in the backwoods of nowhere.

Chapter 7

While they were cooling out and watering off the horses, they pondered together on Bonnie's secret.

"Was it a fluke?" Julie asked. "I know she felt as if she was—well, Gallonette, herself! But what do I know about how a really fast horse feels?"

"*I* know, it's my business. Tuxedo wasn't running at her top form, but she was setting a pace that no other St. Clair racer could have matched. No, Bonnie's a phenomenon. She has the stuff to make a consistent winner. Her stride's long, something between twenty-five and twenty-six feet, I'd say. She's a router. She . . . oh, glory, she's a born and bred racer, Julie! I'd match her tomorrow with, why, with Starless Night herself!"

Julie could not answer him. She blinked rapidly and allowed her jaw to sag. They paused to give the animals a mouthful of water.

"She has to race," Monty said with emphasis. "Julie, it'd be criminal not to race her! A horse this good just would not be happy as a lifelong backyard pet. Besides, she could make your fortune. I know she could." He ran his fingers distractedly through his hair. "But we can't race her, no matter who she is and where she came from, unless we have her registration papers!"

Julie nodded. These papers were filed by the breeder upon the birth of every Thoroughbred foal; ordinarily, they would go with the animal whenever there was a change of ownership.

68

"I'll bet Spire has them," she said. "He seems to sell everything piecemeal; remember that thing he called a halter? He's probably got Bonnie's papers tagged 'Ten dollars, antique document' or 'Genuine Thoroughbred registration, very rare'!"

"Either he has them or he can direct us to her last owner. Are you game to visit the Yard again? We could check this on the phone, but I'd rather see him in person, because I'll be surprised if he isn't holding out on them, and I want to watch his eyes when I ask him about them."

"Sure. When? Today? This morning?"

"As soon as we're through with these two racers."

Two racers, he said, thought Julie proudly. Small prickly thrills were rippling up her arms; she was sure that under her sweater there was a square yard of gooseflesh. A racer, that's you, Bonnie baby.

"A Thoroughbred? What are you talkin' about?" said Spire, scoffing at them in his molasses-in-gravel voice. "That's some kind of fancy racing horse."

"She's a Thoroughbred," said Monty.

"She's just a plain saddle nag. Not that she ain't a fine one, mind; I told you that you were gettin' a bargain. But there's nothing thoroughbred about her. I know."

"The filly's a registered Thoroughbred and she ought to have papers. They must have come with her." Monty was watching the fat, doughy face, but he couldn't read it. Spire's eyes were deepset and they didn't move much, being directed toward some point of interest slightly above the left shoulder of the person he was addressing.

"Nothing came with her, take my honest word, young fellow, she was brung in naked as a hog. Some farmer, said he was from near Zanesville or Steubenville, I forget just which, he brung her here in his truck. Said he had to sell her, account of goin' broke. So I took her. Thoroughbred! He didn't even know who the daddy was."

"And no papers," said Julie sadly.

"Not so much as an old newspaper." Spire scratched his stubbly chin. "I know you're wrong, kids, that's a good saddle horse and not a thing in this world more. Say, did her knee get unswole?"

He seemed genuinely concerned. He's not a bad man, really, Julie said to herself, warming a little toward him; he's just pretty dumb about animals.

"Yes," said Monty, straight-faced, "it unswole fine."

"I'm glad to hear that. She was a nice horse, never even tried to bite me." He turned away. "Sorry I can't produce some kind of papers for you, kids, but it's just that you're all wrong about her. If she's a Thoroughbred, I'm John D. Vanderbilt. And I *know*."

"Well, thank you, Mr. Spire," said Monty. He and Julie got into the car and swung away. "Two possibilities," he said before the girl could speak, "and they're *one*, he's lying his head off, or *two*, the 'farmer' who sold her to him was. Unless the lie started farther back than that. Never mind, we're not beaten yet by a long shot."

"What will we do now?" she asked, hope stirring again.

"Call the Jockey Club. Their registry office has a file of every Thoroughbred in the country."

"You mean they can tell you what her real name is, and—"

"From the tattooed number on her lip. Yes. Then we can get in touch with the original breeder and find out what she was doing in Spire's Original Yard."

"And we can procure her papers and train her and race her and become millionaires."

"Easy does it. I shot off my mouth in excitement when she beat Tuxedo. She may not be all that good, even though I think she's a top-notch filly. But this may be a complicated business and take a long time. And there's always the chance that she was stolen, and we don't have a legal right to her."

"Oh *no!*" Julie yelped. "If they're going to come

and take her away, I'll die, Monty, just die! I'd rather keep her where she'd never *see* a racetrack."

"We'll go slowly. But we have to look into it, Julie. The possibilities are too wild to ignore."

As soon as they'd covered the forty miles back home, Monty was on the phone, Julie hanging on his shoulder trying to hear both ends of the conversation. When the Jockey Club had answered, Monty said, "This is the St. Clair breeding farm, Montgomery Everett speaking. A friend of mine has bought a Thoroughbred without papers, and I'd like to check on it. The lip tattoo is 673954. Could you consult your records for me, please?"

"They'll come and take her away and I'll give up the ghost right at your feet," whispered Julie frantically. Now that he'd initiated the investigation she was torn between curiosity and dread.

At the same time, the man on the line chuckled. "That's one number I know by heart, Everett. But I'll look it up before I tell you why, just in case my memory's failed me." Before Monty could say anything, he had laid the phone down with a clunk.

"What'd he say?" hissed Julie.

"He's looking it up now." What under the wide blue sky, Monty asked himself, could it mean? Why would the man know Bonnie's registration number? Out of the thousands upon thousands . . .

It was Monty's turn to develop gooseflesh.

"I was right, Everett," said the telephone, chuckling in his ear again. "Your friend read the number wrong. The horse that's tattooed with *that* number is owned in Kentucky, and has been running at the tracks—"

"But I read the number myself," said Monty blankly.

"Better take another look at it. I don't know who your friend has, but it isn't the Deepwater Lemon."

"The *what?*"

"Sorry, I shouldn't have said that." The man became contrite. "Very unprofessional of me to laugh, you understand. But that's what she's called in private; a nasty sort of inside joke, but it's been going the rounds since midsummer. You must have heard of the bay filly that brought four hundred thousand dollars last year at the Fasig-Tipton?"

"Of course."

"Great pedigree. She's been running poorly, though —you must have noticed."

"I'm fairly fresh out of the armed forces. I recall the sale, but . . ." Monty cleared his throat, which had gone very dry. "Could you describe the filly, sir?"

"Bay, no white markings, good-looking big filly. You can see why I recognized that number. Her price was the record, of course." The voice seemed to shake its head in wonder. "By Bold Ruler out of Starcrossed. Four hundred thousand. And hasn't finished in the money yet. You can understand why they call her, ah, something of a lemon."

"Yes. Well, I'll check this tattoo again, and thanks, sir," said Monty. Then, as an afterthought, "What's that filly's name?" he asked.

"Star Princess."

Monty cradled the phone and sat there motionless, his expression one of shock and bewilderment.

"What did he *say?*" Julie begged. "I couldn't hear him!"

"He said we read the number wrong."

"We didn't. What else? What else?"

Monty's thoughts went from Bonnie running at full gallop to the $400,000 filly finishing out of the money every time, then to the spare, identical descriptions. "He didn't say much. There's a horse running under that registration number. Star Princess. She brought the record price at Saratoga last year."

They stared at each other. "What does it mean?" Julie said huskily. "If 673954 is Star Princess, why does Bonnie have her number? Who's Bonnie? How can we find out?"

"I don't know. But we *will* find out." He stood up. "Julie, you know what you have to do this afternoon. I won't be here for a while, but you can handle your work, or call on Stash if you need to."

"Where are you going? What about Bonnie?"

"Bonnie will keep a while. Now don't flip out too far, there's likely a simple explanation for the whole thing. Think about something else."

She glared at him. "Men!" she said. "Can *you* think about something else, Mr. Smart Apple?"

"Lots of other things."

"Name one!"

"Oh . . . Catfish, gum arabic, the Parthenon, Poe's raven—do you know that if another kind of bird had stepped into his chamber that night, children in school would be standing in front of the class today and reciting, 'Then with many a crispy crackle, In there stepped a stately grackle'?"

With that he made his escape, pursued by a long wail of frustration from Julie.

Monty realized that he had let himself say far too much today: about Bonnie having the makings of a winner, all that excited stuff; maybe even the Star Princess information should have been kept from Julie. The girl was worked up ("So would I be in her place," he growled to himself), and this was such a baffling tangle of a problem, with no clear-cut answer in sight. . . . He would go slower from here on, not just bleat out the first thing that came to his tongue. He had to remember that Julie was still a girl, and not a calm, mature graduate of the army, like some others he could mention.

I was more hysterical than she was when Bonnie pounded Tux into the track. I must admit it.

He slid into his car again and set out on the well-known road to Spire's Yard.

At first he tried the courteous approach again. Couldn't Mr. Spire give him some further lead to the "farmer" who'd brought the filly in? No, Mr. Spire couldn't. Mr. Spire had given his all for that poor animal, treated her like a member of his own family, coddled and pampered her, and made only twelve dollars on the whole deal if you counted the expenses, which of course any honorable man of business would, and for that sort of miserable profit, he shouldn't be hounded to his grave about some dang-fool paper that had never existed, and when was this uppity snot kid going to allow him to go about his respectable day's work? Or words to that effect.

Well, the only way to handle a vulture is to knock him around, or at least pretend to, thought Monty resignedly. He could talk all week and get no further than this. He eyed Spire narrowly, jutting his lower lip out.

"Spire."

"Yeah?" said Spire, already looking more wary.

"I just got out of the army."

"So?"

"You want to know what they called me in the army, Spire?"

"What?" The fat man was watching him now with real apprehension. Monty surmised that the squint and the thrust lip made him look a little like Bogart, in a wicked role.

"They called me the Butcher." Monty thought it unnecessary to explain that they had done so because of his mild disposition, and the fact that he was always picking up stray dogs and feeding them Grade A beef.

"They did, huh?" said Spire, backing away slowly. "Whaddaya know. Heh heh."

"Spire."

"Yeah?"

"Tell me about that horse, Spire."

The other had now backed right up against one of his tottering shacks. "Well now I just don't exactly know much more'n I already told you, son," he said, making small undecided motions to left and right, his eyes focused on infinity. "Honest, now."

"Spire." Monty reached out a hand slowly and gathered a fistful of coat and shirt and with an enormous effort slid Spire some six inches up the wall of the shack, which groaned and seemed about to collapse behind the weight. Spire's feet waggled helplessly in the air, and his face turned dirty white; he was actually frightened, Monty realized. "Tell the Butcher, Spire," he grated.

"Okay! Pumme down!"

Monty put him down. Then he leaned on him gently. "Go ahead, fat man," he said, doing the Bogart with well-hidden glee. "And remember, I won't *finish* you, if you lie to me." He paused. "I'll let the law take care of that."

"Now, we don't need the law, son," said the terrified Spire, "I'm an honest merchant tryin' to make a buck. Can't blame a guy for that." He was probably a fence, Monty realized, buying and selling stolen goods; and the last thing on earth he would want would be a visit from the police.

"Nobody's blaming you, Spire. Just spill it to the Butcher." His army friends would have been rolling in the aisles by now. He came close to snickering himself, but turned it into a snarl.

"I got her from a guy, used to be a trainer, name o' Zeke Matthews. Zeke dumped her on me and said kill her and burn or bury the carcass, see?" Spire was talking fast now, ingratiatingly. "I looked at her when he'd left and I couldn't do it, Mr. Butcher, I just couldn't. She was a nice horse, I mean like *nice*, and I'm not a butcher—I mean, I'm not mean, you know? No offense! Anyhow, I didn't do it. I got a soft heart."

"And you thought you could make a buck," Monty said, borrowing Spire's phrase.

"Why not? I gotta live. But he gimme twenty bucks to do it and I wasn't gonna argue with him, because he's tough, you know? So I said okay. Then I took care of the horse and she kept losin' weight, I guess she had something wrong with her—"

"You just didn't know how to feed a Thoroughbred. Not your fault," said Monty, feeling a little sorry for the man.

"And when I seen the chance to have a nice little girl take her and give her a good home, I did the right thing." He looked up at Monty, still pale as dough. "Din't I do the right thing, Mr. Butcher? Could any saint done more?"

"You did the best you could," Monty admitted. "All right, I appreciate your telling me the facts. Where can I find Zeke Matthews?"

"Oh, you *wouldn't*," Spire mewed, turning, if possible, a shade whiter.

"Yes I would."

"I don't know where he hangs out, right hand up, sir, I haven't got the least idea where he went when he left, or if I'll ever see him again. Maybe Zeke Matthews ain't even his right name. I only met him onct or twict. But if he finds out I din't shoot the horse, he'll shoot *me*," Spire pleaded. "He's a bad one. I mean real bad news.

"Why did he want the horse destroyed?"

"He never said. I figured maybe he just didn't want her running at the tracks. He got reasons of his own, you can bet on that."

"And why did he bring her to you?"

"I dunno. Oh, I won't lie to you; him and me has had one or two little deals before, sure. But never killin' anything." He wrung his hands. "How did I know that nice little girl would know anything about race horses? How'd I know what I was gettin' into?"

"You didn't." Monty pulled out a notebook and wrote his name and phone number on a page; he tore it out and gave it to Spire. "I'm at St. Clair Farm near Blankton," he said. "If you hear of Zeke Matthews' whereabouts, call me. There's a twenty in it for you."

"Trust me," said Spire, folding the scrap of paper as carefully as though it were a bit of the Magna Carta, and tucking it into his pocket. "Do me a favor, Mr. Butcher, I mean Mr. Everett," he said earnestly. "If you run across Matthews, take care of him, will you?"

"Take care of him?" repeated Monty, scowling.

"Shoot him before he shoots you. And me too," said Spire miserably.

Monty made his gangster face once more. "Don't worry about Matthews," he said, "worry about me." Then he got into his car and tore out of there before he went into a gale of merriment.

If I fail as a trainer, he thought, maybe I'll become an actor. I do pretty well at it. And without a script.

Chapter 8

Spire watched the car out of sight. His mind was going at full speed, which was rather slow and devious. This sinister young punk, who was obviously as stubborn and evil a character as ever hung around a street corner tripping old ladies, was going to dig out Zeke Matthews, that was plain. Something had to be done to hedge the bets in Spire's favor.

He waddled as fast as he could into the house and in his panicky haste fell over a 1908 rocking chair, which had a tag on it stating that it had been Abraham Lincoln's favorite seat. Spire and the chair collapsed on the floor together, and one of the rockers tore loose with a creaky complaint. Making a mental note to change the tag to George Washington's favorite, since it was now a lot more antique than it had been, he scrambled up and got to the telephone. He dialed a number penciled on the wall, and waited. Someone answered. "Gimme Zeke Matthews," said Spire hoarsely.

I'd have give the punk a fake name, if I'd only been thinkin', he told himself. No, I wouldn't of; he'd have found out and come back and tore me apart. I had to tell him it was Matthews.

Spire could not recollect when he had ever felt so oppressed. And all from doing a good deed. He had now convinced himself that his humanity was the cause of it all, and not his desire to earn a dishonest dollar.

"Yeah?" said a voice on the phone.

"Zeke? Sam Spire."

"What do *you* want?" said Zeke, like a tiger speaking to an earthworm.

"Somebody was just here askin' about that horse. You know which one."

"Who was it?" the voice demanded alertly.

"A hooligan from up north. Name of Everett. A very tough guy, Zeke. He's onto something. I thought I better warn you."

"How could he be onto anything? Did you bury that filly deep?"

"Well, that's what I wanted to tell you," said Spire, feeling as if he had lain down, unknowingly, on a very hot stove.

"Tell me, fat boy," said Zeke in a voice constructed of ice.

Somehow Spire stammered and bubbled out the facts, colored a little in his own favor. When he had ground to a halt, there was a long, long pause.

"Spire," said the ice menacingly, "you not only got a sticky palm, you got a head full of Philadelphia scrapple."

"I know, Zeke," said Spire miserably.

"I ought to boil you in lard. Maybe I will. Look, has anybody else been asking about the filly? Did anybody else even *see* her?"

"No one in particular. Leastways, not that I remember. You know how it is, folks in and out all the time," said Spire, recalling that perhaps a hundred people had commented on the horse while he'd had her.

"Yes, I know how it is, you bubble-brained nincompoop. Why did I ever trust such a nitwit? Listen, do yourself a favor: start remembering good and clear before I come up there and scatter those cheap glass marbles you call your brains all over your junkyard! There's more riding on this than you can imagine," said Zeke, seething with audible wrath. "Put a strain on yourself and *think*. Has anyone from a place called

Deepwater Farm, or from the tracks, been there asking about her?"

"I told you, nobody but the hooligan and the girl."

"Nobody named Alex Homer? Nobody who mentioned that name?"

"I never heard of Alex Homer," said Spire righteously, as if that fact were a credit to his own good name. "Who's he?"

"Guy that trains the Deepwater string."

"Zeke, nobody like that ever comes here."

"Okay. Maybe we'll come out of this all rosy yet. Where does your so-called hooligan live? Did you find that out?"

"I got his name and all, sure. He's from the St. Clair Farm. Probably works as their thug."

"St. Clair! Why the blue flaming pit didn't you just sell that filly to Calumet? And Thoroughbred farms don't hire thugs, you porpoise; he's some stable hand— I hope that's all he is." Zeke paused in thought. "Okay. Sit tight and keep your fat mouth shut. Somehow we're going to get that filly back and make certain she disappears off the face of the earth, see?"

"I see," said Spire, not seeing at all. A vision of Monty looking wickedly at him rose before his eyes. "But you ain't took a gander at this guy Everett," he protested weakly. "He looks like—like Humfee Bogart."

"I don't care if he looks like King Kong. He works for St. Clair and he's got my filly. Sheesh," said Zeke between his teeth, "I ought to have my skull examined for trusting you with as much as a burnt match! Listen good, Spire. I'll be there in the next couple or three days. I can't leave now, not if you was to get elected president. But look for me in two days or less, if I can make it. . . . I'll need a big-caliber gun and one bullet. Now get your fat in motion and dig a hole big enough for that horse, and deep enough so nobody can discover it without an excavating rig."

"That's a lot of work, Zeke—"

"You are lucky that I don't make you dig it with

your teeth," said Zeke, in a tone of such hatefulness
that Spire quailed from the phone. "Get this into your
head, too: if Alex Homer shows up, or anybody that
might even vaguely know him, you never saw a horse
in your entire rotten life, Spire, and you don't even
know what one *looks* like!"

"I got it," said Spire faintly, mopping his face with
an oily rag. "I dunno nothin'."

"You can say that again," said Zeke Matthews, and
hung up with a bang.

Spire quivered for an hour. He knew he was in deep
and mysterious trouble. He considered fleeing to South
America.

"I can't do that," he said at last, giving up. "Who'd
take care of the cows and chickens?"

About the moment when Spire decided to face
whatever dreadful music was coming, Monty arrived
home and, avoiding the stable and Julie, went to
his own room and began to call friends and acquaint-
ances at various farms and tracks. In a little while he
had pieced together the following oddly shaped bits
of fact, which gave him no clear picture at all, but
which were, at any rate, a start toward assembling the
jigsaw puzzle that fate had dropped in his lap.

Star Princess, evidently a real facsimile of Bonnie
in appearance, was being trained at Rollin Tolkov's
Deepwater Farm, in Kentucky, by a man named
Alex Homer.

Homer had started out in racing as a small-time
owner himself—a gyp. A gyp in racing is not a
swindler; he is the owner of perhaps one or two
horses, who travels with them, cares for them himself, and lives from hand to mouth, usually because
he loves racing passionately. "Gyp" is an abbrevi-
ation of "gypsy."

Homer had traveled with a trainer named Zeke
Matthews. (Monty had opened his eyes wide when he'd
first heard that; a clue, Watson, a full-fledged clue!
he'd thought.) Matthews was barred from the track

for drugging a horse. No one Monty talked to had any use whatever for Matthews. "A nasty cold piece of work," said one of his friends; "he'd dope his own mother if he thought she could win."

Alex Homer had then taken out his own trainer's license. So far, in spite of the association with Matthews, his record was clean. He did have, however, a reputation for gambling over his head. He was described to Monty as a rather handsome man except for a thick white scar that ran from the corner of one eye down over the cheekbone to the upper lip. More than a year ago he'd lost his last horse in a claiming race, and gone to work for Tolkov, shortly before that gentleman bought the $400,000 filly at the Saratoga yearling sale.

Nobody knew where Zeke Matthews could be found these days. And nobody cared.

At last he hung up and leaned back, thinking. He couldn't find out any more from here, that was clear. He'd been careful not to let any hint of Bonnie's existence slip out, but possibly he'd have to, sooner or later, in order to make progress.

He would say nothing more to Julie about the matter for now; he'd agitated her enough. "Maybe I'll pay a visit to Alex Homer and Star Princess," he muttered. "Man! This morning I was a simple country boy, learning to train horses, and this evening I'm Sherlock Holmes, involved to my ears in The Case of the Scar-Faced Trainer and the Look-Alike Horse." He checked his watch. It was too late to start for Maryland, where they were racing at Bowie. Tomorrow morning, then, early.

He started so punctually that he was there well before noon. He flashed his assistant trainer's card at the gate and entered the grounds of the track. Browsing around the racing barns for a while, until he felt that he had become part of the scenery, he found the stall of Star Princess and leaned on the bottom half of the door to look at her.

There were differences, yes: the Princess had slightly

larger ears, her chest was not quite so wide, and her expression was not so alert and spirited as Bonnie's. However, the coloring was identical, deep rich bay with glossy black points, and the conformation was so close to Bonnie's that only an expert Thoroughbred handler could have told them apart. If Monty himself hadn't seen Bonnie for a week or two, he might have mistaken Star Princess for Julie's orphan filly.

Noticing a jockey watching him in what might have been a suspicious manner, Monty walked off casually to lean on a railing and gaze at various other horses being walked or groomed in the pleasant autumn sunlight. Perhaps his caution was overdone. After all, he had a perfect right to be on a racetrack, in a shed row. . . . The atmosphere of intrigue and secrecy that had enveloped him in the last twenty-four hours was getting to him. He couldn't help it; he was skulking around like an outlawed tout. He did his best to relax and look innocent. But he had the distinct impression that if someone suddenly demanded identification, he would have given them a false name.

A goat, the stallmate of some horse, came up to him and began chewing absentmindedly on his trouser leg. Monty detached it firmly but kindly, and it wandered away. He watched it go, idly, and saw it pass a handsome, tall man with a broad white scar on his cheek.

Monty observed this man, who undoubtedly held some, if not all, of the answers to the mystery; he tried to read his character in his face, and failed. It was like trying to guess what kind of a person a movie actor may be by looking at him in one role.

Alex Homer disappeared into the barn. Monty thought hard.

Time to plunge in and get his feet wet.

Or drown?

Grinning wryly, he assured himself that he could swim. He went to the barn. The scarred man was not in view. He asked a groom where Alex Homer might be.

"Who wants to know?" The groom had obviously

been warned to be careful around nosy strangers.

"Tell him I have a message from Zeke Matthews about a dark bay filly," said Monty. That should rattle Homer, if there was indeed something fishy going on.

"I'll see if he's around," said the groom. "Wait here, Mac." He hustled away.

Monty waited. In a minute the groom came back. "Sorry, Mac, you just missed Mr. Homer. He left a while ago."

"Can I catch him somewhere?"

"He's going on vacation. I don't know where. And I don't know when he's expected back."

Leaving the Bowie track, Monty drove away. He kept his eyes open for a telephone booth. Shortly he found one and put through a long-distance call to the phone in the St. Clair stable. Stash answered. Thank goodness; it might have been his father.

"Stash, I don't have time to go into everything, but I've stumbled onto something that smells a little rotten. And maybe I've stuck a torch under a wasps' nest. I want you to keep an eye on Julie till I get back."

"What way? Like somethin' might happen to that child? She's exercisin' one of the yearlings now," said Stash, concern in his tone.

"I don't want her alarmed, but I don't want her to get hurt, either. And whatever you do, Stash, don't let that filly out of your sight for a minute! I mean Bonnie. Okay?"

"Right."

"I'm coming home as fast as I can. I'm at Bowie."

"Don't worry about a thing, Mr. Monty. I'm on the job."

Monty thanked him and hung up and jumped into the car again. Alex Homer's abrupt vanishing act had startled him badly. On the way to Ohio, he pushed the little car to the speed limit and held it there, reviewing over and over the bits and pieces of his findings and his fruitless conjectures.

The urge to skulk around silently had been the proper one, he thought. That had been a very clumsy attempt to scare Homer into blurting out the truth about Star Princess and Bonnie. Monty admitted that to himself ruefully; he'd been so amused and puffed up by his success with Spire that he'd—well, he'd acted as though he were playing with a bunch of impressionable kids.

From here on, *Butcher,* he said to himself, think things through before you say anything to anybody.

But I'm moving in the dark!

. All the more reason to be careful.

No matter how he turned and prodded at the parts of his puzzle, they didn't make a picture. Not a sensible one, anyway. More like a work of abstract art, he thought. Bit of a horse here, chunk of another one there, a scar and a record price for a filly and duplicate lip tattoos and a fat man selling a filly he was supposed to shoot and . . . Too many people concerned with a horse that was destined for death but saved by an innocent girl. . . .

Well, at any rate, he might as well have put up a neon sign saying that Bonnie the Mystery Horse was now stabled at St. Clair's; so some of the answers were bound to be forthcoming.

Monty hoped they would not be violent answers.

Chapter 9

Stash was waiting for him in Bonnie's stall. He was grooming her elaborately, although Julie had already done it that morning. Luckily, the filly enjoyed being groomed.

"First of all, Stash," said Monty, unconsciously using the other man's favorite expression, "first of all we have to keep a lot of this business from Julie. She mustn't know there's any danger in it."

"Is there?"

"I think so, yes."

"Then you better tell her, Mr. Monty. Otherwise she's gonna walk into it blind, you might say; which is more dangerous than it needs to be."

"But she's only a girl!"

"I don't care for that 'only,' Mr. Monty," said Stash mildly. "That's like sayin' Starcrossed is only a mare. You think 'cause Julie cried a little when this filly was so sick, and 'cause she couldn't knock you down if she hit you, that she's such a puny little cuss she has to be protected from a high wind? Shoo."

"I'm afraid she'll get hysterical."

Stash looked at him over Bonnie's shining back. "Mr. Monty, you know a whole heap, been to school and the army and you're pretty fair with horses, too, but I got to tell you, you don't know the first thing about Julie Jefferson. When the chips are down, she's gonna make

86

you and me look like peeps runnin' from a weasel. No *sir*," he said firmly, "if there's bad things fixed to happen, the first thing of all you do is, you tell Julie."

"Maybe you're right," said Monty reluctantly.

"Sure I'm right. That girl has sand in her craw. She won't do nothing silly or flighty." He bent down to rub the round currycomb hard into Bonnie's side, circle after circle, then dusted with a body brush. "She's over home eatin' her supper now. You go have yours and don't fret about this filly. We'll be here when you get back."

"You have to eat, Stash."

"Had a couple-three sandwiches and some coffee already, and two candy bars and some other little stuff, keep me goin' till we've had our talk," grinned Stash, "but you might bring me back a mouthful of whatever there's too much of, Mr. Monty."

Half an hour later Monty found Stash and Julie sitting on camp chairs in front of Bonnie's stall, with the filly hanging her head over the door listening to them talk. Monty handed the groom a fried drumstick, a wedge of Swiss cheese, and two apples. "I like a balanced diet," said Stash, thanking him. "Julie, you want to give one o' these apples to that hungry little horse?"

"Super. The only thing she likes better than apples is sugar. Monty, Stash says you were at Bowie. What's going on?"

"I'll tell you the whole story if you promise not to get scared."

"I've been living with crazy ideas that don't make any sense rattling around in my head for two days," Julie said flatly. "If you can explain some of them, I promise not to faint away on your hands. Mr. Tough Army Man," she added.

He told them what he'd learned on the phone, what had happened in Bowie. As he heard himself saying it, he half-expected Stash, who was level-headed above the average, to tell him that it was all a medley of nonsense, that Tuxedo had had a bad day, that Monty had been watching too many old whodunits on television.

But it was Julie, trying to be sensible rather than romantic, who said, "Maybe it isn't that Bonnie's so good, but that Tux wasn't putting herself out to win."

"That big mare *always* shove herself to the limit," Stash pronounced. "No, this Bonnie girl, she's so much horse, we ain't seen a half of what she's got in her. I know that ever since she walked out on the track the first day she could get that far."

Together they tried to reason out the riddle. "Let's assume," said Monty, "that we're right, that someone switched horses, that Tolkov has a ringer in his stable. Now who could possibly have worked the thing out? Who stands to make money from a deal like that?"

"You can forget Mr. Tolkov," said Stash. "Grapevine says he's a full-grown Boy Scout, and right in line for a halo. Folks don't come nicer, grapevine says. And you know the vine, if there's somethin' to be told against a man, it tells it."

"Besides," Julie put in, "he paid almost half a million dollars for the filly. He'd only be stealing from himself."

"How about insurance?" said Monty. "The filly was supposed to be killed."

"No insurance if that Spire man puts her down, now is there?"

"No, of course not. She'd have to be put down by an official vet from the insurance firm."

"Or somebody they sent, yep. 'Fore that, she'd have to get examined to prove she was really bad off. Why, even if she was walkin' dead lame, couldn't run ten yards, she'd be worth money—fine stock for a brood mare. Just makes no *sense* to kill her."

"Right. Tolkov has to be out of it. Besides, he's a millionaire, he makes money legally. It'd be crazy for him to pull some shady stunt, fooling around with horses." Monty ruffled his hair wildly. "Who *could* it benefit?"

"Zeke Matthews?"

"He's the first one I guessed, Julie, yes; but that angle doesn't seem to work out either. Why would he take the risk of switching horses on Tolkov and then have the good one, four hundred thousand dollars worth of filly, killed?"

"Revenge?" suggested Julie. "He hates Tolkov. Tolkov, oh, foreclosed the mortgage on Matthews' old mother."

"Can't just say that couldn't be it," said Stash. "We don't know nothing about Matthews. He might have a grudge and be so hot mad about it he taken a chance . . . But it's pretty weak. Findin' a ringer that looks so much like the first filly, then exchangin' them, that cost plenty of cash. Then if he's that wild, and laughin' up his sleeve at ol' Tolkov that he's fixed good—why'd he just give the horse to Spire and say Shoot her? Man that crazy, he's gonna take a gun to the horse himself! Not gonna just hand her over to any old body else."

"We have to suppose that Matthews is in the plot, if there is one," said Monty. "What if someone outside the ring of thieves got onto it? Then he'd get scared and make the horse vanish. No evidence."

They all thought fiercely.

"No," the young man went on, dissatisfied, "that doesn't fit either. There'd still be the look-alike horse to worry about. If anyone were suspicious, all he'd have to do is inform the racing secretary, and half the officials in the country would be checking on Star Princess."

Julie said, "Alex Homer! If that happened, he'd take care of the second horse."

"But that makes killing Bonnie—if she's the real Bold Ruler filly—even more illogical. If Zeke and Alex were working together, and there were outside suspicions, all they'd have to do would be re-switch the animals. Nobody could ever prove anything then."

" 'Sides that," said Stash, "it's four months we've had Bonnie here, and prob'ly five or six since Matthews taken her to Spire's. Somebody suspicious about the deal would have done somethin' by now, wouldn't they? The Princess wouldn't be runnin', she'd have melted away like a piece of ice on a hot pavement."

They looked at one another, baffled. "All I know is, either you or I, Stash, has to have that filly in sight every minute until something pops."

Stash nodded his head soberly. "It's gonna pop, too, I can feel that in my bones. That Homer fellow talkin' right now to Spire or Matthews, you bet good money on it. That message you sent him must o' spooked him bad, or he'd seen you."

"It was a stupid trick to pull," said Monty.

"Maybe not. How else you gonna flush out your birds? Looks to me like we could have investigated till Bonnie grew a long white beard and not found out something that's hid away in the heads of maybe only two men, and them thinkin' she was buried. No, sir, you *had* to throw a scare into 'em. You did fine."

"I hope so. All right, I'll collect a couple of blankets and be right back. I'll sleep in her stall tonight. Julie, better go home and get to bed. We never know, it seems, when we're going to have a long day."

"I want to help guard Bonnie."

"Don't blather. Don't you trust me?"

"Yes! I only want to help. But okay," she said, "I promised not to be any trouble, and I won't. Can I tell Dad about this? No," she answered herself, "he'd worry. Good night, then, Monty. Be careful, please." She took two steps and came back and said seriously, "It keeps going around in my head and I was afraid to say it out loud, but if Bonnie is really Star Princess, and we prove it, we'll prove that she belongs to Mr. Tolkov. What chance will I have then to keep a four-hundred-thousand-dollar horse? I'll *lose* her." They all stared glumly at one another. "So think good thoughts about her *not* being Star Princess," Julie said, without much hope, and turned and left the stable.

"She forgot to say 'night to Bonnie," said Stash. "She's worried. But she'll hold up like steel, you'll see; and she's safer now she's on her guard, Mr. Monty."

"Yeah," said Monty, "right. You were perfectly

right. I have to start remembering that Julie's grown up."

He went off for his blankets, Stash whistling something behind him. It took him a few moments to place the tune. It was the Wedding March.

Monty felt his cheeks actually reddening in the cool darkness. Ah, come on, Stash! he thought. She isn't that grown up!

Well, gosh, almost.

It was the middle of the night when he woke, and for an instant he had no idea where he was. Then he remembered—Bonnie's stall. He'd bedded down there to protect her. Monty sat up, noting that the filly was standing, looking out over her door.

What had wakened him? He'd heard something, a creaking noise. That was it. Bonnie nickered, shifting her weight from hoof to hoof, and backed farther into the stall; something was making her fidgety. What had creaked? He watched Bonnie as he listened intently. The big shadow across the stall neighed again softly. Beyond that he caught the sound of wood groaning. The door at the end of the aisle was sliding open, very gradually. One of the other horses answered Bonnie, then a third. They must all be awake.

Monty moved as quietly as the crackling straw would let him to the front of the stall, crouched against the wall there, and waited. The wonderful memory of the horse had already determined that the steps, stealthy and almost inaudible to the man, were those of a stranger; and like all her breed, Bonnie distrusted and was wary of anything unknown. She said so again, stamping, and the others repeated her observation up and down the row.

Monty saw a light on Bonnie's head, shining very faintly and then disappearing. He could not guess what it was. Then it came to him: the intruder was using a pencil flashlight to look at the horses, or to read the name cards above the stalls, on the other side of the aisle. It was reflecting dimly from Bonnie's burnished coat.

He waited, tense and impatient, wishing that he'd thought to bring some sort of weapon to bed with him. Belatedly he realized that anyone who'd have a fine horse killed might not hesitate to use violence on a man. Well, he'd count on surprise to disarm the fellow, if he were indeed armed at all.

He heard the trespasser reach the end of the opposite row and start down past the empty stall to Tuxedo's, pause an instant, come on. Then a slim beam of light shot over Bonnie once and went out. Monty gathered himself to pounce. The catch clicked open. The door swung outward. The shadowy figure of a man stood in the entrance. Monty squinted hard at him; he could make out very little of the face, but he would have sworn that it was not the hawklike profile of Alex Homer, Tolkov's trainer. It was a flat sort of face, he thought, and the man was not as tall as Homer.

One step inside and I'll jump him, he thought, waiting.

Bonnie, who was watching the stranger with her head high, interfered.

With a shrill, long scream of panic, she reared and came down with her forelegs driving at the man in the doorway. He leaped back, making an angry and frightened sound halfway between a grunt and a curse. Monty unwound, pushed past Bonnie, slammed the stall door behind him. The other man was halfway toward the end of the aisle, having taken off as soon as he'd realized that Bonnie was not alone. Monty sprinted after him, the terrified whinnying of horses in his ears.

The man was squeezing through the partly open sliding door into the main part of the barn. Monty was within seven or eight feet of him. The dark figure snatched up a pitchfork and slung it hard and viciously at Monty. He felt it slice into the calf of his leg with a searing pain, and fell sideways as the stranger bolted down the barn.

Monty struggled to his feet and limped after him. He had vanished now. Monty headed for the door, flung it wide. In the blackness outside, he heard an engine roar to life, then the crunch of wheels on the gravel drive. The car was moving without lights. Monty clawed hastily for the light switch, losing precious seconds before he found it and flooded the courtyard with white brilliance. He staggered outside and strained to focus on the rapidly disappearing vehicle. Below the dim outline of a horse trailer, he saw the license plate; he could not distinguish any figures, but he would have sworn it had the black and white coloration of a Virginia plate.

Then it was gone.

He stumbled back inside. No use getting out his own car. He didn't even know which way the stranger had headed when he'd hit the road.

The barn lit up around him, and his father said, "All right, Monty, what's going on around here?"

Monty hobbled over to his side. Will Everett was dressed in green pajamas, red slippers, and a blue-black Colt .38 revolver.

"I'll tell you all about it in a minute," said Monty, gritting his teeth against the pain, "but first, Dad, have you got a Band-Aid in your pocket?"

Chapter 10

Julie looked at her father over the rim of her glass of milk. "Bonnie?" she repeated. "She's fine, she's just wonderful." Why had he asked about the horse in that peculiar tone?

"I mean, what's going on behind my back, with that filly at the center of everything?"

"Oh. I wasn't supposed to tell you, but if it's that obvious, I will." Julie felt far better than she had before; this was the first time she'd ever kept anything of importance from him, and it had disturbed her. "It started when we found out that Bonnie could race like the wind, two days ago," she began.

Rand Jefferson held up one hand, smiling. "All right, honey; I know all about it. I guess you didn't hear the phone ring, about two thirty this morning?"

"No," she said blankly.

"You sleep like a stone these nights. If you weren't so hound-dog healthy, I'd worry about you working too hard."

"The phone," she said. "Who was it? Is Bonnie safe?"

"And sound. It was Will Everett. Monty'd told him the whole thing."

"And he called you about it at two thirty in the morning? We didn't think it was *that* important," Julie said. "Or I guess we did, but—"

94

"But you didn't care to have the old folks prying around, spoiling the fun for you. *I* know. I was young myself, a zillion years ago. No, Bonnie had a visitor last night, and Monty took a pitchfork in the leg, protecting her. He's fine," said her father hastily, as she cried out and put a hand to her mouth. "But Will wanted old Doc Jefferson to look at the wound, me being a lot closer and more amiable about getting up at night than the doctor in Blankton. The tine gave him a shallow, pretty painful stab in the muscle of his left calf. He's probably up by now and walking with a limp, but I cleaned it out well and he'll just have an interesting scar in a few days. Really, Julie, it isn't bad at all." He poured coffee. "He and Will and I had a long talk about your mystery. Decided quite a lot."

Julie's heart settled down glumly somewhere around her left boot. She waited.

"We decided, for one item, that there's no use alerting the Blankton police department, because it consists of two men and obviously neither of them could be stationed permanently at St. Clair's."

"Check," said Julie.

"We further concluded that somebody has to play night watchman, because as long as Bonnie's there and the enemy seems determined to get her or do away with her, the whole place is in danger. Will Everett is going to put one of his men on the first trick, and I'm going to take the late hours till five thirty, when the horses wake up and the grooms come on duty."

"But you—"

"Oh yes I can. You don't want to cut me out of all the fun, do you? Kitty's going so well at the store that I can trust her to handle things while I take a week's vacation. However: if anything further happens at St. Clair's, we'll have to notify the State Police; we all decided that was only right."

"Sure. We never thought anyone might be in danger, except Bonnie."

"As to Bonnie, now. Will and I are leaving her to you and Monty. Oh, and Stash, who'll take turns sleeping in her stall. Will admits that if he forbade it, Stash would just overrule him, so as long as regular work isn't interfered with, you three have your heads, to solve your riddle however you can."

"Oh, Dad!" Impulsively she swept around the table to kiss him on the cheek. "You're a grand guy to have for a father, you know it?"

"I'm a model papa," he agreed. "How about showing me Bonnie's far-famed running abilities today? I've been eager to see her since the glowing description last night. Seems she beat Tuxedo."

"Ran her into the ground," said Julie proudly.

"And you can handle her, as a jockey? You've learned a lot over there, haven't you, girl?"

"I've had two great teachers, Dad."

"You certainly have. Happy?"

"Yes! Except I'm worried about Bonnie, naturally. I don't want Mr. Tolkov coming around saying she belongs to him."

"Maybe that won't happen. We don't know *what* will happen, honey, so let's take one day at a time and not fret. You finished with breakfast? Then let's go see your horse."

They drove to St. Clair Farm in the car. As Julie was getting out she saw something move under the car robe in the back seat, and yelped with surprise.

"That's not your horsenapper," said Rand, his brows drawing together, "but I think it's a criminal, all right." He flipped aside the robe. The raccoon blinked at them drowsily. "Hello, Burglar. I had a suspicion you'd been bedding down back there. Smelled a little raccoony yesterday." He drew a fold of the cloth over the sleepy little beast. "I've raised a houseful of characters," he said. "Life would surely be dull without 'em, though."

He accompanied Julie to the stable, where Bonnie greeted her noisily. The filly was none the worse for her alarm of the night before. Julie put the tack on her and led her out. They went through the brisk clear morning to the track, where the girl hand-walked her for ten minutes to relax and loosen her muscles and joints.

Julie mounted and settled herself, and said, "Okay, Dad, watch her and you'll see something really beautiful." Off they sailed. Stretching out her fine head low and eager, Bonnie pounded down the track, the great hindquarters rocketing her forward. Rand, who knew more than a little about riding himself, watched his daughter, noting the taut and well-handled reins that assisted the filly in her drive instead of hampering; the stillness of her body as she sat barely moving at all, just letting her filly work; all the things she knew that he hadn't known she'd know. . . . The girl was turning into a rider, a genuine rider. And, he thought, almost as an afterthought, that is *some* horse, too.

Here they came. Rand wished he'd brought a stopwatch. They—he included Julie as an essential part of what was running out there—they were incredible. Even going alone, with no running mate for comparison, they seemed to be skimming along at championship speed.

The thunder of hoofs continued for perhaps a mile. Then Julie brought her down and finally stopped before him. "How'd you like her?" she asked, breathless.

"I liked her. I liked both of her."

"Thanks, Dad."

"You were right, she has a fantastically beautiful gallop," he said, and was going to go into detail when it happened. Bonnie threw up her head, shrieked loudly, and reared, far up, so far that she seemed in danger of falling over on her back and crushing her rider. Automatically, Rand started toward her, realizing that he would not be able to grab the bridle before the horse had bolted away.

Julie had leaned forward to meet the rising neck, and kicked free of her stirrups. She had not anticipated anything like this sudden rear, and acting from instinct, did what Stash had taught her to do years before: flung her arms around Bonnie's neck, as far as she could reach beyond the withers, and as Bonnie came down on her four feet again, threw herself off the saddle on the left side and swung her body forward and away from Bonnie and released her hold on the neck, slamming into the ground heels foremost, so hard that she fell flat on her back. Bonnie raced away down the track. Rand Jefferson bent to lift his daughter.

"Okay, girl?"

"Think so. Oh," she said breathlessly, "is she all right?" watching the horse tear around the curves. "What spooked her?"

Rand, satisfied that Julie was unhurt, glanced behind him. "There's the culprit!" He put Julie on her feet and took a couple of steps and picked up the raccoon. "Had to see what was going on, did you, Burglar? You —you blame scalawag!" He cradled the little black-masked beast in his arms. "Bonnie has obviously never seen a raccoon before. And what a horse hasn't seen, he'll run from. That's Jefferson's Law. Passed by Act of Congress in 1947." He had been badly scared by the bolt. Julie could have been injured; but she knew that as well as he did, and there was no sense making it worse for her. He was talking to calm her and himself.

"She'll jump the fence. She'll hurt—no, she won't," said Julie, as the filly, shaking her head, cooled down quickly and came trotting across to them. "There's my good little horse, oh, there's my brave girl," said Julie, still breathless, half-laughing with relief. "She was only startled, weren't you, baby?" Bonnie nuzzled her, apologizing.

"Where'd you learn that trick?"

"What, sliding off? Stash dinned that into me when I asked him to teach me to ride, back when I was a little kid. Before he'd even put me on a pony, he made me practice that. I hadn't thought about it for ages."

Bonnie stepped forward slowly and extended her head to sniff at the raccoon in Rand's arms. Then she backed away, snorting. Burglar eyed her disdainfully, wriggling, wanting to get down. Then the horse very gradually approached it again and, full of curiosity, smelled it loudly. Burglar, intrigued in spite of his customary aloofness, put his own head out. They touched noses briefly. Each of them satisfied, and

Bonnie reassured, they lost interest.

"I wouldn't have jumped off," Julie said, "but I wasn't certain I could stay with her if she really started moving. She might have dropped me. At least, I *think* that went through my head while it was happening. Funny. You're never really sure afterward, are you, of what you thought?"

"That's true. You probably went on sheer instinct. Want to walk her while I put this gentleman safely in the car and roll up the windows?"

"See you at the stable." She walked down the track leading Bonnie, and her father, looking after her, stroked Burglar, thinking that Julie's mother would have been very proud of her at this moment, as proud as he was. Not for what she'd done, but for how she'd taken it. In her stride. In her brave little stride.

"Some girl," he said to the raccoon. "But I hope she doesn't have to lose that horse. I don't know how she'd take *that*. Because that's really important to her."

He put Burglar in the car, allowed him two inches of open window for comfort, and went to find Will Everett.

Monty emerged from bed quite late in the morning and limped down to the stable leaning on an old blackthorn cane that had belonged to his grandfather. His calf was stiff rather than painful. He was sure that by the next day he'd be able to drive without much trouble.

He found Julie, busily engaged in cleaning Dovewing's stall. The big gray stallion was out being exercised by Stash. Monty waved aside her expressions of sympathy about his injury.

"Don't you ever pause?" he asked her, grinning. "Sit down and play a harmonica, or swap tall stories with the other guys? Just loaf a little?"

"This is more fun."

"You're more my father's child than I am. Do you clean house the same way?"

"Silly. This *is* cleaning house."

"Hey, Julie," he said seriously, "I've been thinking. You know we haven't any choice now, we have to press on and find the truth about Bonnie."

"I know. I'm scared."

"It doesn't necessarily mean you'll lose her."

"If she's Star Princess, or vice versa, I probably will. If that happens, you know what? I'll go and be a groom for Mr. Tolkov."

"I wouldn't put it past you. Anyway, when I saw that trailer last night, I knew Bonnie was in real jeopardy and that I have to dig fast and hard to discover what's what. I'm willing to bet that one Zeke Matthews was the man who put that pitchfork into me."

"Why?"

"Because it wasn't Alex Homer. He had a kind of flat face, and he wasn't as tall as I am. As far as we know, there are only two of them involved in this. Besides Spire, and that sure wasn't fat Sam who came here last night."

"If it was Zeke, where do you suppose he is now? Waiting for tonight to . . . to strike again?"

"No. He'll know we'll post guards, for a while anyway. So he probably went home to wait a week or so. I'm only guessing, but I think it's likely he's in Virginia by now, sweating."

"Why Virginia?"

"The license plate was from there. He'll be living not far from one of the tracks."

"I thought he was barred—"

"Yes, but a man like that who's spent most of his life around racing won't be far away from it. He'll always be thinking that he'll be able to get in again—because racing's all he knows. Of course you realize, Dr. Watson, that this is pure theory, but based on acute observation and amazingly intelligent deduction."

"Yes, but it makes sense anyway."

"Don't be insulting. Whatever I say always makes sense. So tomorrow I'll head for Virginia, pausing for a minute at Spire's Original Thieves' Market to throw another scare into him and try to find out more about Matthews."

"Virginia's a pretty big place. Bigger even than Blankton."

"But there are only so many tracks. When I've covered them, I'll try the breeding farms. No I won't," he corrected himself, "because I'll get lucky at the first or second track."

"Pompous."

"No, a hunch. My luck is as the luck of ten, because my heart is pure. Tennyson, abridged."

"Monty, be careful. I'll be worried about you."

"Now, Julie, don't be anxious! All I have to do is find Matthews someplace where there's no pitchfork handy."

"All right. And you aren't to fret over us, because Stash and Dad and —gosh, I guess just about everyone at St. Clair's will be keeping their eyes on us."

"That's the only reason I feel I can leave you here," he said soberly. "Oh, and please don't work Bonnie while I'm gone, just let her gallop."

"Why?"

"As Stash says, we haven't seen more than half of what she has in her to do on the track. And if she got away from you, took a strong hold and really flew, she could buck her shins or pull something or have trouble with the rail on the turn and pile herself—and you—up. Okay?"

"All right, I won't. We'll canter sedately round and round. I never thought about *her* being hurt."

"And don't get out of sight of Stash or—"

"And you stop fussing, Mother Hen!"

"I'll try," said Monty.

Chapter 11

He headed southward at the break of dawn. In less than an hour he was banging at the door of Spire's den. The fat man, in a robe that was a genuine antique, opened the door and saw him and tried desperately to close it again. Monty shoved it wide.

"Give," he grated.

"What what what?"

"You told Zeke Matthews I'd been here. You told him where to find me." Monty hefted the blackthorn stick, scowling. "Don't bother denying it, Spire. I know."

"Well, he called me, see," said Spire, backing across his living room (if you could call it that), fiddling with the frayed collar of the bathrobe, "and he says has anybody been askin' about the horse—"

"Don't lie to me, Spire. You ought to know better."

"So I called him! Sue me!"

"No, I'll just ask the cops to grill you a little. When I'm finished."

"Now, now, Mr. Butcher, sir, no need for them to get into this. Sure I called Zeke. I'm scared of him, and that's the plain truth." Spire's face indicated that it was, indeed, true. "I knowed he'd guess about me talkin' after you'd caught up with him. So he came up to try and steal her."

"So that was Zeke. I thought so."

"Then he went home, when he seen the horse was protected." Spire retreated behind a dilapidated davenport. "And I don't know where he' lives, honest! Except," he added reluctantly, "it's in Virginia someplace. That's all I know. And I ain't real sure o' that, but his car had Virginia plates, see?"

"I see." This was probably all true, thought Monty. "All right, I'll take your word. For now. But if you call him again, if you tell him I've been here, I will do things to you that do not bear thinking about," he said coldly. "Keep your nose clean, Spire. This is serious now. You got that?" he demanded loudly, causing Spire to duck behind the sofa.

"Yeah, yeah, I got it. Trust me."

"Not with a counterfeit penny," said Monty, and left the place behind, to take off southeast for Virginia.

Two days and three tracks later, he had almost run out of ideas on likely hangouts for a character like Matthews. He had been in and out of fifty shed rows or more; he had reconnoitered six or eight racetrack cafeterias; he had lost count of the number of lounges, bars, poolrooms, and recreation centers he'd canvassed; the stream of faces he had talked to seemed endless. No one had admitted knowing one Zeke Matthews. Monty began to wonder whether he'd come on a wild-goose chase.

There remained three or four places to investigate in the area of the third track. Monty decided that if nothing turned up, he'd check in at home before visiting the fourth and final track in Virginia.

By early afternoon he was growing disheartened. No such person as Zeke Matthews, ex-trainer, ex-horse-drugger, had ever impinged on the state of Virginia. He'd stolen that license plate. He'd gone to earth in Louisiana. He'd changed his name and had plastic surgery on his face. He'd . . . oh, what was the use?

Monty turned in at a neat little restaurant and bar about three miles from Shenandoah Downs. The place was empty; the regular clientele had not yet begun to drift in. The barman, a chatty soul, was acting as waiter. He welcomed Monty's company and horsey conversation. Monty, leading gradually around to the subject of his quarry, thought wryly that he was becoming an expert at the game. At last he said, "Ever see a fellow around here called Zeke Matthews?" after he'd asked after several friends of his who existed strictly in his imagination. The barman grunted.

"Have I!"

"Oh? Lately?"

"He used to eat here regular. Haven't seen him in over a year, though." As Monty's faint hopes perished, the barman chuckled. "Funny you askin' about him today, though. Small world."

Monty's hopes gave a small chirping noise and revived. "Why?"

"I guess doping horses is a win ticket in this week's popularity contest. Somebody else asked after old Zeke just yesterday."

"For pity's sake," said Monty mildly. "Anybody I'd know?"

"Big good-lookin' geezer with a scar on his face like somebody took an axe to him one time. Say, you aren't a friend of *his,* are you?"

"No," said Monty truthfully. "Never met the .gentleman. Thanks a lot. I mean, for the service and talk. Got to pull out now." He tipped the barman freely and took off, mind racing. So Alex Homer was after Zeke, too!

And he didn't know where to find him, either . . . but he was looking in this vicinity!

Better keep after it for a while, boy, he told himself.

He worked his way toward the fourth track, buoyed up by his unexpected success. From a scrap of news here and there, although he came no closer to news of Matthews, he found that Homer was searching just as hard, about one jump ahead of Monty himself.

All the roads turned out to be dead-end streets. Deciding at last that he was only wasting time, that for some reason Matthews had been avoiding tracks for a year or more, he gave up and drove home. Besides, his leg was paining rather severely; he had likely given it too much exercise. He stopped in Blankton to let the local doctor check it over.

"How'd you do this?"

"Pitchfork."

"Ought to be more careful around sharp things, son. Stay off the leg for two or three days."

"But I have a lot of work to—"

"You have a lot of walking to do on that leg in the next sixty years. Rest it. That's an order. How's your dad?"

"Just fine, thanks."

"He's too blame healthy. I never see him. Give him my best."

Monty went home and, stretching out comfortably in Bonnie's stall, told Julie and Stash about his meager accomplishments.

"Don't seem much chance, short of a fluke, to locate either of 'em just now," said Stash gloomily. "What're we gonna do, Mr. Monty?"

"We can't ask our fathers to keep patroling the farm day and night," said Julie firmly. "It's too much to expect."

"That's true. I thought it would all be over by now."

"Me too," Stash agreed.

"There's only one thing to do," the girl went on. "I'm scared, but we have to do it. We have to see Mr. Tolkov."

Monty agreed. "But I have to stay off this leg for a while. Maybe we ought to telephone him."

"That isn't the same. Who'd listen to a story like this on the phone?" Julie took a deep breath. "I'll go to see him," she said.

"Better make a 'pointment first," Stash told her. "Mr. Tolkov is a busy man, 'cause he's a millionaire and they keep busy. First thing of all, Mr. Monty calls him, says he's from St. Clair Farm, can his associate Miss Jefferson have a 'pointment to consult on a racin' matter. Then you go, Julie."

"Good idea," said Monty. Before either he or Julie

could develop cold feet, he hobbled to a phone, looked up the number in his listing of farms and tracks, and dialed it. After going through various secretarial barriers and bogging down with a dead line for agonizing minutes, he reached Rollin Tolkov, repeated Stash's formula, listened, said Thanks, and turned to Julie, hanging up the instrument.

"Can you be in Kentucky by noon tomorrow? Near the Lexington area?" She nodded. "That's good, because I said you would be. I'll write down the route for you," he said. "I have a feeling from what all those secretaries said that your engagement is from twelve o'clock to twelve three, so you'll have to talk fast."

"Does he sound very frightening?"

"No," Monty said. "He sounds like a nice fellow. I think maybe the grapevine's right about him."

"The old vine's never wrong," said Stash, "except when it makes a mistake."

"You can take my car," said Monty. "I won't be needing it for a few days. And practice your speech on the way."

"Don't worry," she said, "I'll be too nervous to think of anything else."

And promptly at noon the following day, Miss Julie Jefferson, in the dress that made her look older than she was, and in a state of considerable terror, presented herself at the door of Mr. Tolkov's office on Deepwater Farm.

"Miss Jefferson! Come in," said Rollin Tolkov heartily, standing up behind his massive desk. He was a heavyset man, somewhere in his fifties, with a neat gray beard and twinkling eyes; she liked him instantly. "What can I do for you?"

He listened quietly to her story and her ultimate, stammering conclusion that she believed—that just about everyone at St. Clair Farm believed—that the real Bold Ruler filly, the $400,000 filly, was at this moment stabled near her home, having been bought for $200 out of a river, skin and bones and destined for a quick, violent finish.

He smiled. It seemed to Julie a cooler, more wary smile than he'd given her at her entrance. "How old are you, Miss Jefferson?"

"Seventeen?" said Julie on a rising inflection, as though she were asking him if it was all right to be so extremely young.

"And who sent you here?"

"Why, nobody, we just decided, Monty and Stash and I, that there wasn't anything else to do but talk to you. It was my idea, I guess, originally."

"Yes. Well, I don't know what horse you have, and the lip tattoo does suggest some kind of plot, but I can assure you that Star Princess is the filly I bought, no question of it. Here, look at her registration papers." He produced them from a file drawer and handed them across the desk to her. Julie realized that either he considered her a very silly girl with a head full of fanciful notions, or else he suspected her of pulling something shady, to get registration papers on a horse that had none.

She looked down at the papers, noting the breeder of the Bold Ruler filly; she knew it was useless to pursue the matter now, no matter how stout and jolly Mr. Tolkov was. "Thank you, sir," she said. "It is a terrible muddle. I don't know what to do next."

"If your horse is in danger, and it seems she is," he said kindly, "I suggest you go to the police."

"Thanks again," said Julie sadly, and took her leave.

She hurried out to her car, nodding to two secretaries on the way, and digging out a notebook from the glove box, wrote, "Monroe Bradley, Fieldstone Farm, Versailles, Kentucky," before she could forget it. That was where the Bold Ruler filly had begun her life. Maybe there'd be some answers there. At least, it was worth a try.

Versailles was only half an hour's easy drive from Deepwater. The post-office man gave her instructions on how to find Fieldstone Farm. "But it's closed, you know," he said.

"Closed?" There went the heart, sliding into the boots again. "Isn't anyone there at all?"

"Just Bill Morehead, he's in charge of the estate. I hope you weren't looking for Monroe Bradley, child? He's dead these three months. You kin to him?"

"No. I want to find out about a horse that was bred there."

"Bill might be able to help you."

Bill Morehead tried. He had been in Monroe Bradley's employ for forty years, and knew everyone who'd ever worked on Fieldstone. Looking at Julie, sensing her anxiety, he polished his spectacles and thought hard. "Best man for you's Leon Pitt. He was head stud groom till last year, when the stable was disbanded. He's retired now," said Morehead, "but you shouldn't have any trouble finding him. He lives somewhere on the outskirts of Southern Pines."

Julie repeated the name dubiously.

"It's in North Ca'lina," said Morehead. "I don't know the street, but you can find it easily. Everybody in town probably knows Leon Pitt. His family's been there for generations, I remember him talking about it."

"Every place is so *far*," said Julie, "and there's so little time," she added, thinking of Bonnie's danger. "All right, thank you very much, Mr. Morehead."

"Just wish I could be more help. But Leon will be, you'll see. He knew that foal better than her mammy did. I recollect he used to call her Gum Drop."

"He knew her till she was sold to Mr. Tolkov, then. How about after that? Would he have seen her or—"

"No, Leon retired when the yearling sales were over, last year."

"Well, I'll try him," said Julie resignedly. "Good luck with Fieldstone Farm, sir."

"I hope we sell the place soon," said Bill Morehead. "I'm going to retire myself then. Good luck to you, too, young lady."

She walked from the big house, glancing around at the stable, the exercise track, the outbuildings, all well kept up, although with the curious atmosphere of long emptiness that grows about any such place when it is merely tended, not used. Even with her spirits cast down, Julie could admire the beauty and the intelligent layout of the untenanted farm. My Bonnie was born here! she said to herself. She must have had a lovely first year.

Suddenly she wanted very much to meet the man who'd known her horse better than anyone else had. The man who'd affectionately named her Gum Drop. Southern Pines seemed a lot closer than it had five minutes ago.

It was then, she realized, that she accepted the idea as fact: Bonnie *was* the Bold Ruler filly. There was no doubt of that at all in her thinking. Bonnie was, or should have been, named Star Princess. Bonnie had once been Gum Drop. Bonnie . . . Bonnie of Fieldstone Farm.

Why was she, unexpectedly, so certain of it?

No reason at all that Julie could ever spell out to herself. She simply absorbed the air of the place and breathed in with it the knowledge, the absolute and astounding knowledge, that this was where *her* filly had been born. So fine a horse had to have come from so fine a home.

Suddenly, Julie simply began thinking of Bonnie as Gum Drop *and* Star Princess *and* Bonnie, without even noticing the disappearance of her uncertainty.

There's a meadow where she played, rolling on her back with her thin young legs stuck up in the light wind. There's a pretty little pool where she drank. There's the stable where she had a stall.

Smiling, Julie got into the car and headed east-southeast for the home of Leon Pitt.

Chapter 12

"Hi, Monty. I'm sorry about reversing the charges, but I'm not sure I have enough money with me. You can take it out of my wages."

"Don't be silly. Julie, where are you? I didn't catch what the operator said."

"I'm in a motel about a mile from Southern Pines. That's in North Carolina."

"What are you doing *there?*"

"In the morning I'm going to see Mr. Leon Pitt. It was too late by the time I got here. I lost my way and . . ."

"What about Tolkov? Why North Carolina, for gosh sakes?" he demanded irritably. He had been worrying over her for hours, and was immensely relieved to hear her voice, perky and obviously all right.

"Mr. Tolkov didn't believe me. So I went to Versailles, where Bonnie was born, at Fieldstone Farm. And it's for sale, but a man there told me—"

"How do you know Bonnie was born there? Julie, you're talking shorthand. Tell me the whole thing."

"I was just trying to save on the phone bill," said Julie, and traced her trip for him from Deepwater Farm to Southern Pines. "And that's all so far. How's your leg?"

"Much better. When are you coming home? Or are you going to visit New Orleans, as long as you're down South anyway?"

"That's a really neat idea, but my money won't last that long. Don't worry about me, Monty. And I'll call you after I've seen Mr. Pitt. 'Night," she said, and hung up. She ate a hamburger, took a shower, and piled into bed, where she lay awake, unable to turn off her thoughts, until midnight; then the long drive caught up with her and she slept like a rock until eight in the morning.

She had no trouble locating the Pitt residence. "Why, land," said the first woman she asked, "everybody in town knows Leon Pitt!" which was what Bill Morehead had told her. Ten minutes later she was knocking at the door of a neat little white-painted house, and two minutes after that she was sitting in the living room, under an enormous print of Gray Majesty, the mighty Thoroughbred champion, who had been bred at Fieldstone many years ago.

"Offer you a little tea, Miss Jefferson, before we talk?" asked Leon Pitt.

"Oh, thank you, I'd love a cup."

He smiled and nodded to his wife, who vanished and reappeared instantly with two huge steaming mugs. "So Mr. Morehead sent you to me. What do you need, Miss Jefferson?"

She leaned back and felt herself relaxing. This gentle-spoken dark man gave her confidence, with his level, friendly gaze and the strong, economical movements of his body as he walked and gestured. She said, "It's about a filly you called Gum Drop."

He flicked her with his eyes; she could not read the expression, but his voice was full of tenderness as he said, "I loved that foal. Maybe better'n any of the others. And you know what they call her now?"

"Star Princess."

"The Deepwater Lemon," he said bitterly, and that explained his curious look of a moment before. He was genuinely grieved at what had happened to his darling. "I don't know why she's not runnin' proper, Miss Jefferson, but I know one thing: it ain't her fault.

That was the biggest-hearted yearling ever left Fieldstone Farm."

"I believe you, Mr. Pitt."

"Please," he said, smiling, "just Leon. Everybody in racin' calls me Leon, and you're from St. Clair Farm, so you must be in racin' yourself, right?"

"In a small way. I'm assistant to Monty Everett, who's an assistant trainer."

"That'd be Will Everett's boy," said Leon; Julie was to discover that he had an entire racing encyclopedia and who's who in his head. "You know Stash Watkins, then," he added.

"All my life!" said Julie, amazed.

"Good man."

"He's super!" exclaimed Julie, and restrained herself with difficulty from going on about Stash and Monty. "Leon, about Star Princess—she isn't Gum Drop."

He leaned forward in his chair. "Go on."

"That's why she isn't racing well. She's a ringer. I have Gum Drop in a stall at home."

He was looking at her so hard that she did not continue. At last he glanced down at his powerful forearms. "Look at that," he said mildly, "goose bumps." He eyed her again. "You know, Miss Jefferson, I believe you. Even before you tell me how come, I believe you. It's the only thing makes sense o' what Star Princess is doin' on the track. Now you tell me."

Julie told him, from the very beginning. He winced at her description of the filly's condition when Julie found her; a frown deepened between his eyes as she continued, and at her account of Bonnie outrunning the top stakes winner of the farm, he slapped his knee and shouted for joy.

"She beat Tuxedo? That's Gum Drop, that *has* to be Gum Drop!"

Julie went on to tell him about the tattoo and everything that had happened when they'd begun making inquiries about Bonnie. When she had finished explaining how she'd been sent here from Fieldstone, he was quiet, sipping his tea, for several minutes. Then he spoke, almost like a man speaking in a dream.

"You call her Bonnie. That's a fine, fine name for my sweet Gum Drop, Miss Jefferson. I like that."

"Please, everybody in racing calls me Julie."

He chuckled explosively. "Okay, Julie. Look at this." He stood up and unhooked a tiny halter from its place on the living room wall. "You'll enjoy seein' this, I bet. This is her first one. I put it on her myself when she's six days old. Mr. Bradley's people, they gave it to me when I asked 'em."

"You loved her as much as I do," said Julie, touching the little scrap of leather and feeling sentimental.

"Would you like to have it?"

"I'd rather you had it, Leon. Her first year belonged to you."

He hung it up. "Well now. If Mr. Tolkov, he don't believe you, why are you so set on provin' Bonnie is the Princess? You know it means you probably lose her," he said.

"She's in danger until we discover what's going on with Matthews and Homer. Besides, she—she deserves her heritage."

"Oh," he said softly, "you are real horse folks, Julie."

"And it wouldn't be fair to Mr. Tolkov, either, if she was stolen. He paid an awful lot of money for her."

"He sure to goodness did. And he sittin' there in his house, stubborn as three mules, sayin' No, no, that ain't my filly. I guess we have to show him he's wrong, for his own good, poor man," said Leon Pitt. "So I'll come out o' retirement long enough to see this through. If you don't mind a busted-down old-timer throwin' in his hand with you?"

"I'd be so grateful," said Julie with relief. "But you aren't an old-timer, Leon."

"Be sixty pretty soon."

"Which is too young and restless to be moping around the house, Leon, and you know it," said Mrs. Pitt from the kitchen.

Leon laughed. "Forty years at Fieldstone Farm made me think I was ready for the pasture, but I do get feelin' unquiet, you know, 'thout a horse to look after. Julie, you ever notice any scars on your Bonnie?"

"Only the ones she got at Spire's. And they healed well."

"On the inside of her, lemme see, her *right* elbow, if she's truly Gum Drop, there's a scar. When she was just a baby, she fell on a rock in the field. I stitched her up right away, did a good job, too," he said with the rightful pride of the professional, "but the hair grew in white for about an inch, and there's a little tiny bump where I had a drain. It's hid good, in the folds of her skin, but it's there, you can find it."

"I've got to call Monty," said Julie, jumping up. "Can I use your phone? I'll reverse the charges."

"Right over in the corner there. I'll just see if Mary Anne has somethin' like a biscuit or cornbread or somethin' we can nibble on," said Leon, and went into the kitchen, his feet fairly bouncing on the carpet with the pleasure of this new episode, interrupting a life that seemed now to have become far too placid and uneventful.

She got Monty's father, who accepted the collect call in his customary gruff style. "I suppose you want to speak to one of the two other musketeers," he said. "Hang on." Monty was on the line shortly. She described the scar to him, and he dashed off, to return in a state of much excitement.

"It's there!" he fairly shouted into the phone. "This is the real—"

"I knew that," Julie said, rather smug. "Monty, I think Leon, that's Mr. Pitt, is coming north with me. He knows Bonnie better than anybody else, and he wants to help us."

"Great. Now Tolkov will have to listen."

"You know," she said, suddenly very sober, "I'm almost bound to lose her now. My Bonnie."

"We'll fight for her, Julie. I don't know the law, but you bought her fair and square." He paused. "We'll see.

Meanwhile, come on home, and by all means bring Mr. Pitt if he's willing."

"He'll be willing. It was his idea to throw in with us."

"Yippee," said Monty, "another good guy! Drive safely." And he hung up.

Monty Everett stood by the telephone, thinking hard. A matter of only a few yards from where he was at this very moment, four hundred thousand dollars' worth of horse nickered softly. Prepared though he'd been for the possibility, he was still shaking slightly with excitement.

Stash came in, leading a yearling. "You had some news," he observed, "and I bet it was from Julie."

"Leon Pitt identified Bonnie for her. By a scar."

"Leon Pitt? He was Monroe Bradley's head groom. He retired a while back there. And so Bonnie's the Princess. My, my," said Stash, who had not known of Julie's call the night before, "Julie gonna be shaken up a lot at that. I wish she din't have to drive herself all the way from Kentucky."

"Kentucky? She's in North Carolina!" Monty told him. "But she'll be coming back with Leon, he'll look after her. Stash, I'm brewing up a scheme."

"Count me in."

"You bet I am."

Stash put the yearling into its stall. He started to groom it quietly. Monty came and rested his arms on the half-door. "I believe I have it, Stash. How does this sound?" Rapidly he outlined his plan.

"Not bad. Sounds like a movie, a little, but I've seen wilder notions work out. You want to tell your dad, or shall I?"

"I'll explain it to him. If I get his go-ahead, I'll call Tolkov. This time I bet he'll listen to us," said Monty grimly.

"He'll listen," said Stash. "Anybody knows the first thing about racin' knows Leon Pitt's say-so about a horse is *it*, period. Even a great big millionaire has to know a thing like that."

"Man, I hope so! He was pretty cool with Julie."

"He thinkin' Julie's some little girl with a saddle pony, that's all. Leon Pitt, he's another kettle o' mash entirely. Mr. Tolkov, he'll listen hard when you say 'Leon Pitt' to him."

Which, to Monty's surprise, Mr. Tolkov did.

"Well," said the bearded man slowly, after a lengthy pause, "that does sound convincing. Mind you, I'm not *entirely* convinced, Everett. But my natural skepticism suffers a blow when Pitt identifies that scar for you."

"He hasn't seen it yet, but he's on his way here now."

"I admit that yesterday I thought that girl of yours had a head full of fantasies, or worse. But I asked some of my people about you. Your family has a fine old reputation in this business—so does St. Clair, obviously. So let's say I'm verging on conviction, and I certainly wish I knew the truth of the matter."

"So do I, sir. That's why I'd like to lay a trap, with your permission. And your help," Monty added swiftly. "You can't lose, no matter how it turns out; if my bait doesn't tempt the quarry, both horses will be safe, and if it works as I think it will, we'll be spared the bother of a long official investigation that might get nowhere."

"Go on," said Rollin Tolkov. He listened without injecting a word while Monty set forth his plot in detail. Then he laughed quietly into the phone.

"Sir?" said Monty, afraid that to someone like Tolkov the idea might have sounded like a melodramatic farce.

"Excuse me for the merriment, Everett. I was just picturing Alex Homer's face when—oh, boy!" said the millionaire, "maybe you'll think it's pretty juvenile of me, but I love it!"

Monty wheezed gratefully. He had been holding his breath till it pained him. "Thanks," he said.

"Promise me one thing. I want to be in at the finish. I'd hate to miss that."

"I promise."

"Then I'll fix up the necessary intrigue on this end, and look for you down here as soon as you can make it." He laughed again. "Between ourselves, son, I never did care much for Alex Homer. He never seems to smile. Don't put your trust in a man with no sense of humor. He'll swindle you every time!"

Leon Pitt and Julie arrived that afternoon. She introduced the retired groom to Monty, Will Everett, Rand Jefferson, and Bonnie, as they encountered each one on the path from car to stable. Leon walked around the big bay filly once, smiling. Then, fishing in his pocket and bringing out half a dozen gum drops, he held them out to her. Bonnie sniffed at them, then nibbled them off his palm. "See?" he said to Julie. "You were right. That's my baby." He inspected her right elbow, though he hardly seemed to think it was necessary. "Certain sure. I'd swear it in court." He looked into the great brown eyes. "I don't s'pose you recollect Leon, that brung you into this tough old world, Gum Drop?"

"She does," Julie said eagerly, "she does!"

"Or else she's glad to taste her favorite treat again," grinned Leon.

Stash appeared. "Hey there, Leon."

"Well, now, Stash. Been a long time."

"Good to see you comin' out of the mothballs," said Stash. They shook hands. "Leon and me, we know each other from 'way back in the days of, lemme see, Gray Majesty, wasn't it?"

"Yep. When he all but taken the Triple Crown—"

"But he pulls up lame in the backstretch—"

"Man! You know how long ago that was, Stash?"

"Oh, we're a couple of old wrecks, indeed, Leon."

"In the backstretch, where?" demanded Julie, who was intrigued by the partly told tale.

"Belmont. That was his picture, Gray Majesty's, you saw down at my place. I raise him just like I raise this fine girl here."

"Did a good enough job both times, too," said Stash. "Look here, Mr. Monty, you told 'em your plans?"

"Not yet."

"Better hurry, then; there's still enough daylight to get plenty of road behind us."

"Where are we going?" asked Leon.

"Down to visit Mr. Tolkov," Monty said, "with Bonnie."

"All of us?" asked Rand Jefferson, perhaps a bit wistfully.

"Leon and Stash and I." Monty smiled at him. "We hoped you wouldn't mind guarding the stable another night or two, sir, until Zeke Matthews finds out for certain that the bait's gone."

"Happy to do it. I enjoy the night air."

"Wait a *minute*," Julie burst out. "What about me?"

"You aren't coming."

"Do you mean that after all this hullabaloo, flying back and forth, stewing about Bonnie's welfare and losing her and everything, that you think for one minute, Montgomery Everett, that you'll just pat me on the head and set me in a corner and take off for the far corners of the earth, having all the fun and finishing the whole job while I sit here and—and—and take up needlepoint?" she demanded. "Think again, chum!"

"If there's anything dangerous going to happen in Kentucky," said her father, "that's exactly what Monty means."

"You can't come with us," said Monty, "because you're going to the track at Kandahar Park, and raise the worst disturbance that ever hit the place."

"I am?" said Julie blankly. "Oh." What in the world did *that* mean?

Chapter 13

At eight the next morning, Julie presented herself at the gate of Kandahar Park, the fairly new one-mile racetrack that lay thirty-odd miles from Tolkov's Deepwater Farm. Showing her identification, she was admitted and went, not to the big complex of buildings, but to the stable area. It was then about three hours before the finish of the working day; the place was boiling with activity. Julie wound her way among horses, jockeys, grooms, attendants, exercise boys, trainers, hot-walkers, chickens, cats, goats, dogs, and all the paraphernalia that accompanied the exercising and care of the racers. She buttonholed an important-looking man and asked him, in a voice three notes higher than her usual tone, "Can you tell me where the stall is that they're holding for St. Clair's Bonnie?"

The man gazed at her as though she were three feet high with lollipop smears on her face. "St. Clair isn't running anyone here today."

"She's shipping in tonight. There has to be a stall reserved for her." Julie turned up her volume. "Gee, they surely aren't going to just let St. Clair's Bonnie stand around in the aisle!"

"I don't suppose they are," said the man, backing off a step. "Why don't you check with Max McGraw? You'll find him down there in the office at the end, see?" He pointed. "But I don't think St. Clair—"

119

"Of course they are. Her name's Bonnie. A big bay two-year-old filly. Ask anybody." Julie lowered her voice to normal, thanked him, moved in the direction he'd indicated; veered off to an area some distance away, and repeated her performance, this time with a groom.

When Monty had explained to her what she must do, her first thought was of the terrible embarrassment she would suffer, making everyone in hearing range stare at her while she acted like a hysterical, spoiled brat who'd never been near a racetrack. Now she found that her mind was so full of Bonnie—the danger of losing her, as well as the peril that Bonnie herself was in until this affair was ended—that making a fool of herself didn't bother her at all. By the third performance of *Julie Jefferson, Girl Blabbermouth*, she had her role down pat. She had now covered most of the territory outside the shed row that formed the central part of the backstretch, and going into the stable, walked down the aisle reading the names over the stalls and asking everyone she met where Bonnie's was. Past a tack-room was an office where Max McGraw sat in solitary splendor, shuffling papers. She went in, repeated her lines in low key, and the large brown man looked up at her and roared "I never heard of a horse called Bonnie!" . . . Then he slowly gave her a knowing wink, and returned to his papers.

Mr. Tolkov had prepared the way. He was really behind them.

"I'll get to the bottom of this if it takes all day!" Julie shouted; she walked out and headed for the buildings over beyond the homestretch.

She found the offices of the state racing commission's representatives, and said to the first secretary, "I want to file my horse's papers. She's shipping in tonight."

"Take a seat," said the girl indifferently.

Julie sat down, fidgeted for a minute, and then said loudly, "It's Bonnie, from St. Clair, and the papers haven't arrived yet—"

"They haven't? Then what are you doing here already?"

"Well, they don't have a stall ready for her, and she's coming down this evening."

"Are the papers coming with her?" the secretary asked blankly.

"No, Daddy's bringing them tomorrow."

"But you can't bring a horse onto the grounds unless its registration papers and race record are filed with the commission."

"She doesn't have a race record. She hasn't raced yet," said Julie, almost shouting, hoping that they'd just think she had a rather loud voice. Everyone in earshot had to catch what she was saying. The word had to be spread.

"Miss, are you sure this horse is from St. Clair Farm?"

"Certainly she is. Bonnie," said Julie, wondering how long her throat would hold out.

"And where is St. Clair Farm?" asked the other girl.

"You believe I'm some dumb kid with a horse out of nowhere, don't you? It's near Blankton, Ohio, just like I am," said Julie.

"The racing commissioner will see you now," said the secretary, probably because she couldn't stand the racket any longer.

Julie went into the inner office and did the whole bit once more. The man behind the desk smiled at her, and said, "Miss, ah, Jefferson, this is highly irregular." Then she demanded a stall and he said that was impossible, and she began working her voice up again, and he shouted at her irritably. All the time they were smiling at each other. At last he beckoned her to lean over the desk. "Great," he said quietly. "I hope when this is all over, you'll tell me the whole story someday?"

"That's a promise." said Julie under her breath.

It went like that all morning. She never knew who was going to be expecting her, having been alerted to her arrival by Rollin Tolkov. Sometimes she demanded

a stall from men who plainly had no inkling of any plot,
and these considered her (and sometimes told her that
she was) a nut, a child who knew nothing about racing,
some kind of weird new tout, or a plain crook. Once she
was halfway to the entrance, being towed by a redfaced
steward who swore that he'd boot her off the grounds
personally, when they were stopped by the racing secretary himself.

"It's all right, Tom, this is being looked into. Let her
go."

"If you say so, Jack. But I think the girl's—"

"We think the papers may be all right."

"But there *aren't* any papers!"

"There may be. We'll wait a while."

It was only when they both gave her tight little
hidden grins that Julie realized the truth: they'd set this
scene up themselves. Tolkov had a long arm.

By noon she had seen three stewards, the racing
secretary, two men from the state racing commission, a
dozen office girls, the clerk of the scales (by accident),
the paddock judge (who happened to be in one of the
offices when she entered, so she took advantage of
that), and practically everyone in the clubhouse area.
She went back to the shed row and spread the word a
little further, accosting passing strangers and saying
huskily that here she was, with her great horse coming,
a beautiful dark bay, sixteen-one, and the papers would
be here tomorrow but they didn't want to give her a
stall, and she thought that was pretty creepy of them,
how about you? The passing strangers consoled her,
avoided her, or laughed at her, according to their na-
tures.

When her voice finally gave out on her, so that she
felt she really had to rest it, she went back to the office
of Max McGraw. She made sure that no one was
around, shut the door, and plunked down in a chair. He
chuckled at her expression.

"Feel like you just sang a couple of grand operas,
Miss Jefferson?"

"All the parts," Julie said, "even the basso."

"You can relax. If there's anyone on the track who hasn't heard about the kooky girl with the big bay filly, he's stone deaf. Everybody's laughing about it. You've done fine."

"Do you know what's going on?" she asked curiously.

He shook his head. "Jack Lillie, the racing secretary, told me that Tolkov, the fellow who owns—well, of course you know him, I imagine—Tolkov asked us to play along with a girl who'd be here making an unholy uproar about her horse. We were supposed to give you a hard time for a few hours, and then reserve a stall for your filly. Near the front door of the stable. Tolkov said it would help to catch a couple of bad actors who were out to dirty up the racing game."

"That's true."

"Well, none of us like to see racing with mud on its face. This is a great sport and a lot of good fellows are giving their whole professional lives to keep it that way. So the stewards said okay, even though the horse doesn't have papers, so long as you weren't going to race her. That's all I know. Must be a sight more to it than that?"

"There is," said Julie fervently.

"Could you tell me about it?"

"This afternoon, maybe? I'm starved now."

"There's a good cafeteria across the track, just past the rec hall going toward the nursery course. It won't be crowded now—it's lucky, by the way, that they aren't racing today, or your story wouldn't have been spread so widely. Tomorrow, that's going to be a big day."

"I'll come back when I've eaten. I feel silly now," she said, "all those people staring at me like a freak."

"Consider that you've given a noble performance, and the stares are your silent applause," said Max McGraw kindly. "Look at the stall nearest the door, by the way, as you go out. There's a temporary sign on it, in black crayon on white paper you could see for a mile."

There was. It said BONNIE, *St. Clair Farm*. A tall

handsome man was reading it as she passed. He had an ugly white scar down the side of his face. Julie shuddered all the way to the cafeteria.

She'd known that Deepwater was running horses here at Kandahar this week. She hadn't known for sure that Alex Homer would be with them. The last they'd heard of him, he'd been searching frantically for Zeke Matthews.

Which added a crazy angle to the mystery of course: what had happened between these two, to cause Zeke to make himself scarce?

She hoped she'd find out the whole truth soon—with no danger to Bonnie. She could hope fiercely, but she couldn't know about that.

Well, Homer had the news by now. Would Matthews get it?

Julie was not certain she wanted him to get it. He was too quick with things like pitchforks. And he'd wanted Bonnie under the grass and out of the world.

When she'd eaten, and told Max McGraw the whole tale, after pledging him to secrecy, she drove back to her motel and stretched out thankfully on the broad low bed. She wouldn't sleep, she was too excited; and she had to be back at the track by sundown. But after driving all the way from home before sunup, and throwing every ounce of energy into her sustained acting, she was bone-weary.

It was quite impossible for her to close her eyes. She'd just rest . . .

Julie fell asleep. The sun went down and the brief twilight faded beyond the window. She rolled over, groaned, and went on sleeping.

Monty and Stash arrived at the track at dusk. They were driving a small three-horse van belonging to St. Clair Farm. Directed by a guard to the stable area, they located their barn by questioning half a dozen men—all of whom knew exactly where Bonnie of St. Clair was to be stabled—and led the big dark bay filly down the ramp and into the compartment. They busied themselves making her comfortable until no one was around; then they hustled across the aisle and into the stall opposite. Here they sat down, out of sight, and waited for the full dark.

It came, but no other humans did. Not even Julie, who should have been here to greet them. As one hour, then two, crept past, Monty grew more worried about her. She was too brave for her own good; maybe she was out there now, doing something like shadowing Alex Homer; or maybe she'd tried it and been caught. Monty chewed a knuckle miserably. "Where you think she is?" he whispered.

"Sssh," Stash cautioned him. "She'll be okay."

It wasn't like her not to keep an eye out for them here, though. It was nearly eight o'clock. A man came into the stable, whistling softly, and passed down the rows of stalls out of hearing. Then another man walked in, so quietly they scarcely heard him, and stopped; and the sound of a doorlatch being lifted was clear in the silence.

Monty rose and looked across the aisle. The light was dim enough, entering through the open door and filtering back, too, from the far end of the stable where a nightlamp glowed. But Monty, eyes accustomed to it, could see plainly.

Alex Homer went quietly up to the filly, who was standing at the back of her stall, and put a hand on her jaw. Monty tensed. Homer raised his other hand and lifted the horse's lip. He was checking the tattoo.

The moment of truth, thought Monty.

Homer gave the horse a mechanical sort of pat, lacking in enthusiasm, and leaving the stall, went out into the night once more.

Where was he going? Had he guessed . . . it was possible. Yet how on earth *could* he have guessed?

Monty crouched and told Stash in a whisper what had occurred. "He's gone for a trailer," said Stash comfortably. "You'll see."

"He knows horses. Star Princess especially. And if he suspected—"

"Not that light in here. 'Sides, right now he's too knotted up with worry to think clear. And in the last place," said Stash with assurance, "this whole thing is so tangled and messed around that nobody could put together any piece of it and be right, not at this here minute."

"You can say that again," whispered Monty, and sat down.

Where was Julie?

Where was Zeke Matthews?

In about ten minutes he had his answer. Zeke Matthews was at Kandahar Park, Kentucky. The word had reached him. He was here.

When they heard a car's engine beyond the open door, heard it purr up and stop, Monty believed that Alex Homer had returned for the filly. This time both he and Stash rose to watch, their backs bent, standing in the thickest shadow of the empty stall. Cautious footsteps approached the barn. A short man with a flat face came hesitantly into the place, his eyes, used to the glare of headlights, blinking hard. He looked directly at Stash and Monty, then on down the row. Monty could hardly believe that they had not been seen. But Matthews moved slowly past them, walking warily on the balls of his feet.

Not glancing left, he missed the glaring white sign, and went almost to Max McGraw's office before turning and coming back. Homer had known just where to head; Matthews obviously had only heard that Bonnie was in this stable somewhere.

Spotting the sign, Zeke came back toward it. He reached into his hip pocket, and Monty gathered himself to burst out of the half-door if Zeke should draw a weapon. Maybe I should have come armed, he told himself bitterly; I thought they'd only try to steal her, not—

Zeke pulled out a handkerchief and mopped his face.

He went to the stall, glared at the filly, nodded with satisfaction, and put his fingers on the latch.

"Well, Zeke! Imagine you being here!" said Alex

Homer. Monty twitched with surprise, but Matthews nearly fell down in his amazement, clutching at the top of the door as he whipped around to face the newcomer.

"Didn't they tell you at the gate?" Homer asked him, grinning. "Men who drug horses aren't allowed on the track."

"Hello, Alex," said Zeke feebly. "I was hoping you'd be here."

"The sun's gonna rise in the west tomorrow, too. Will you tell me, fast and short, Zeke, how this filly got out of your barn and into St. Clair's and then here?" demanded Homer, walking forward. "And where you've been for the last six or seven months?"

"Why, I've been around, Alex," said Zeke, edging back along the front of the stalls.

"I've been spreadin' word I wanted to see you all over Virginia."

"I never got the word."

"But you got the word that the Bold Ruler filly was coming here. Tonight. The word that only got passed today. Right?"

"Friend of mine here let me know, yeah." Zeke was recovering from his fright. He had stopped backing and was now moving toward the other man, very slowly.

"How'd you lose her? Talk, you ape."

"Didn't exactly lose her. Misplaced her for a while." He was about ten feet from Homer. "Gave her to a guy I know in Ohio to take care of—" He stopped talking, and moving, as he stared at what Homer held in his right hand.

It was a small black Colt revolver, with a long black silencer attached to the barrel. It was aimed at Zeke's flat face.

Chapter 14

Julie woke up with a start. The motel room was in darkness. She yanked on the light and looked at her watch; it had stopped. She grabbed up the car keys and dashed outside. The sun was thoroughly gone for the day, but the moon had not yet risen. That made it anywhere from six thirty to eight thirty! She'd slept for hours!

She drove toward Kandahar Park, her mind racing. Monty and the others would have arrived with Bonnie ages ago; he'd be worried sick about her. She'd really blown it, lying down to "rest" when she'd been that tired.

I even forgot to wind my watch this morning. What a conspirator I turned out to be.

She drew up at the closed gate to Kandahar and jumped out to show her identification to the guards on duty. Jack Lillie, the racing secretary, was sitting in the booth drinking coffee. "Hi there," he said, smiling at her. "Fellow I think you may know just went in a few minutes ago with a horse trailer on a hitch behind his car."

"Who?" asked Julie.

"He had papers proving up to the hilt that he was John Renard, an agent for the Phipps stable. But I know Zeke Matthews when I see him."

"He's after Bonnie!" she yelped. "He'll steal her and kill her!"

"Easy does it," said Lillie, patting her shoulder. "He's the reason for me being here. Rollin Tolkov asked that we let him in, if he showed up—but he won't get out unless he vaults the fence."

"He'll kill her in her stall!"

"Even a vicious no-good like Matthews has better sense than that, Miss Jefferson," he said kindly. "That would mean a jail sentence—supposing he hadn't been stamped into a jelly by half the men on the track before the police got him. He'll try to bring her through here with his forged, or stolen, papers. And he won't get past us. So don't be afraid for your horse."

"What about Alex Homer?" she asked.

"Tolkov's trainer? He's on the grounds somewhere, unless he went out before I arrived. Is he in on this with you?"

"Not with us, no. I just wondered if you were going to stop him if he tried to leave with a horse."

"No, no instructions like that," said Jack Lillie, watching her with an odd expression. "Should I stop him?"

"I don't know their plans, only what they told *me* to do. I guess not," she said reluctantly. "I'm sort of baffled, you know?"

"You can imagine how *I* feel," said the racing secretary.

"You wouldn't shoot me," wheezed Zeke Matthews, glaring at the gun. "They'd catch you sure."

"Don't be a fool. I'll be long gone. Nothing to connect you and me, Zeke—I haven't seen you for almost a year. The gun winds up in a swamp."

"You're out o' your mind, Alex."

"I won't shoot you if you behave. Tell me fast what happened to this filly. You left that farm you rented, with her, about March, didn't you?"

Zeke wet his lips, backing off as Homer came up and opened the door to the bay filly's stall. "Yeah. There was a guy always hanging around, looked like a cop to me, maybe a private investigator. I got scared, sure; who wouldn't? I took her to a friend of mine in Ohio to keep for us. And he goofed. Got greedy, sold her to some girl that turned out to live at St. Clair Farm."

Monty, tense and poised by the unlatched gate of the stall across the aisle, wished he could yell out to Zeke that he was a liar. Alex Homer saved him the trouble. "You don't make sense, Zeke. You're leavin' things out." He moved into the stall and took the horse by the mane; he led her to the aisle, still holding the gun on his ex-partner. "Put that halter on her. Talk while you're at it. What crummy scheme did you work out—and how'd it go wrong?"

Reluctantly, Zeke haltered the horse. "It's the truth. Okay, I had cold feet, but so would you have, if you'd been sitting on a farm about three yards square with a hot horse! That so-and-so kept hangin' around." He turned to face Homer. "I found out later, when I saw him at Churchill Downs, that he'd been trying to get a job on a breeding farm near my place. On the square. But how was I to know that, anyway? He looked like he'd turn me in for fifty cents, and every time I went in town, there he was."

"So you panicked," said Homer coldly.

"You would too in my spot! With my record, a four-hundred-thousand-dollar nag in my barn, and you—you in the clear! I couldn't have proved nothing on *you*," said Zeke bitterly.

"So you decided to double-cross me." Alex led the filly to the entrance, Zeke following. "How'd you sell her without papers?"

"I tell you, I didn't sell her!" shouted Zeke.

"Keep your voice down, you meat-head."

They went outside. Monty and Stash slid out of the stall and hurried to the doorway, to watch the horse being urged up into a trailer by Homer, who somehow managed to hold his gun on Matthews as he wrestled with the reluctant animal. He got her in and disappeared with her, no doubt attaching the chains to her halter rings. All the time he and Zeke were arguing back and forth, but so quietly that Monty could not catch a word.

Homer reappeared, dropped to the ground, and began to raise the tailgate. Zeke made his move, rushing the tall man, his arms outspread like a charging gorilla's. Alex Homer twisted around and with a motion so slow and easy as to look absolutely casual, lifted the gun and fired. The silencer muffled the sound to a dull *whump*. Zeke pitched over backward and lay still.

Monty would have run out, save for Stash's iron grip on his arm. "We go out, we'll get it too," the groom whispered.

"He may be dying!"

"Nothin' we can do for him if he is. Have sense, son."

Alex Homer got into the car and started it, glanced around at the deserted stable area, and drove off toward the gate. As soon as he was far enough down the length of the backstretch not to be watching in his rear-view mirror, Stash and Monty dashed to the fallen man.

"Why, he's nothin' but cut a little along the ribs," said Stash, shaking his head. "Musta fainted. You want me to call a police ambulance for him?"

"Please, Stash," said Monty. He looked up from the unconscious Matthews at the sound of a car coming faster than usual down the darkened stretch toward them. Alex Homer again? No, it was Julie's car. She shot out of it feet first, almost the instant it came to a halt.

"Monty!"

"Everything's fine. Don't panic."

"I saw Homer with a horse trailer—there was a horse in it—it must have been Bonnie—and they're going to let him through the gate!"

"I hope so. You see—"

"But Bonnie's gone! She's kidnapped!"

"It isn't—"

"I tell you I saw him! Who's this? What about Bonnie?"

Monty took her firmly by the shoulders. "Bonnie is fine. She's at Deepwater with Leon. That was Star Princess, the celebrated ringer and look-alike filly. Satisfied?"

"But when Homer discovers that—" Julie began, switching her concern from one horse to the other with hardly a blink, "there's no telling what he'll do to her!"

"Julie," said Monty.

"But—"

"Julie!"

"Yes, Monty?"

"Cool it!"

"Oh," she said, "all right. Man! Who *is* this? He looks hurt."

"Not badly. It's Zeke Matthews."

She stepped back warily. "Oh, him. What happened?"

"I'll tell you as soon as we've got him comfortable on some straw. Stash is phoning for the police now."

"I'll take his feet if you take his head," said Julie practically. They carried him in and laid him on the unused straw of the first stall on the right, where Monty seemed to have spent the last couple of nights and days, crouching and waiting for the enemy.

Stash joined them, accompanied by Max McGraw. "Well, that's Zeke, all right," said the latter, clicking on a light over the stall. "Your act worked, Miss Jefferson." He looked around at them, his large sunburnt face imploring as he asked, "Can I be told what it's all about, now? Before I go raving mad?"

Julie introduced him to Monty, mentioning that he was as up-to-date as she herself was. Monty said, "If Zeke wakes up before the police take him away, maybe he'll fill in the blanks; but I think I know most of it now."

"This scratch ain't gonna pester this man more than a couple days," said Stash, who had knelt to cut away the bloodstained shirt from the wound. "He just got a fearful, quakin' heart, 'spite of being a mean miserable tough guy. I'll wake him for you." He went out and came back with a bucket of water, which he thoughtfully tilted over Matthews' face. The mean miserable tough guy spluttered, gagged, sat up, and choked out, "Don't shoot!" Then he gaped at the four people surrounding him. "What happened? I didn't do anything!"

"Except steal a horse, order her shot, pitchfork this boy, and break all the laws left and right," said Stash severely. "Mr. Innocent. I bet they even framed you on that horse-dopin' charge."

"Sure they did," said Zeke, touching his ribs and cringing. "Look here, I been hurt! You got to get me a doctor!"

"First you tell us about the Bold Ruler filly," said Monty.

"I could bleed to death."

"Just talk till you pass out, then," suggested Monty. "Wake up, Matthews: we don't like you much. Cooperate."

"He needin' more water," said Stash, tilting the bucket.

"What do you want to know?" asked Zeke glumly. "Homer's gonna blab when they catch him, anyway. I got nothing to hide. It was all his idea."

"Tell us how you switched the horses, and what happened afterward. And remember," said Monty, "I know Sam Spire, and he talked a lot about you."

Zeke gave him a sour look. "Yeah, you must be the one he thought was a hired thug. That Spire. He's at the bottom of all my troubles."

"I think you are," said Julie. "You—you horse-thief!"

He gave her a dirty glare; Stash dribbled a little water onto his head. "Okay! It was Homer's idea. He started in training her as soon as Tolkov had her. She was class, real class. He got itchy fingers, he wanted to own her. It was the first time in his track career he'd had to work for somebody else, and he didn't like it. So he and I, we started out to hunt for a double."

"There hasn't been a ringer in big-time racing for forty years," said McGraw contemptuously. "It was a fool's idea. You couldn't have made a success of it."

"We could have, we could have," said Zeke, plainly lamenting the dear days of yore when a man could make a nice dishonest living on the track. "We found a double for her on a farm not fifty miles from Deepwater. I mean, look, solid bay, no markings at all—why, Thoroughbreds like that are forty bucks a dozen. We turned down two others before we found the one we used. Took her to a vet who'd been barred from the track—"

"What's his name?" asked Max McGraw.

"I don't talk about anybody that doesn't double-cross me," said Matthews. "That don't go for Homer; he shot me, didn't he?"

"He did," said Stash calmly. "He thought he slew you good."

"The vet did the lip tattoo on your ringer," Monty prompted.

"Sure. Then one night we switched them, and I took the Bold Ruler filly to a little farm I'd rented in Virginia. We were going to keep her hidden till Tolkov—"

He broke off, and was silent so long that Monty said, "Well, go ahead."

"How do I know you're going to catch Alex Homer? And if you don't, I'm handing you my head on a silver plate. This wound must have knocked the sense out of me."

"You're only filling in unimportant holes for us," said Monty patiently. He outlined what they already knew, speaking rapidly and confidentially.

Zeke lay back and looked at him. "All right, you're onto it. Homer figured that Tolkov could be persuaded to sell off a bad loser, no matter how terrific her blood-lines were. Tolkov was brand-new to racing; he had no breeding plant, he just wanted his horses to *run*. We'd keep the good filly hid, and the other, the Princess, she'd keep losing. She'd run for cheaper purses all the time, then end up in a claiming race after Homer had worked on Tolkov to get rid of her for whatever she'd bring. We'd enter a claim for her—"

"Great day in the mornin'!" said Stash. "Then switch again, and you'd have a four-hundred-thousand horse for maybe eight to ten thousand."

"That's it. So she'd race for us and start to win. And Homer would tell Tolkov that she'd just found her stride, you know, and no matter how much he suspected, he could never prove anything."

"Because the Princess would be in a hole someplace the day after you'd claimed her," said Julie. "Oh, you're a *wicked* man."

"There's worse than me," said Zeke indifferently.

"So then," said Monty, piecing it together from what he'd overheard that evening, "you got scared, thought you were being spied on, realized you had nothing on Homer, and went to Ohio, where you decided, probably after almost dying at the idea of all that money down the drain, that you had to dispose of the good filly."

"On the nose, kid. Put yourself in my place. I was in line for a long stretch up the river if they caught me with her. You can see, I couldn't prove a thing on Homer, but he wouldn't *have* to prove anything on me; *I* was the one with the filly and the bum record. So I figured, if he doesn't know shes' gone, I wait a while till he's ready to make the switch, and I tell him okay, buster, but first I want to see some money."

"Why didn't I deduce that?" roared Monty, slapping his forehead. "I should have seen that a week ago! You were keeping out of Homer's way, trying to finish the job on Bonnie—you were going to blackmail him for every cent the traffic would bear, then disappear, while he waited forever for his good Thoroughbred to show up. And he'd have had to pay, too, because he was in no position to let out a peep."

"You got it."

"Take the cash and let the credit go," quoted Max McGraw. "You miserable skunk."

"You watch how you talk to a dying man," said Zeke severely. "I could sue you."

"Miss Julie, she kinda put a burr under your saddle when she advertised all over creation that the twin to Star Princess was alive and out o' your hands," Stash said. "You must have a pal hangin' around Homer, keepin' watch on him, and he let you know about Bonnie comin' down."

"I'm not saying another word," said Zeke Matthews. He groaned, hollow and phony. "I'm a badly hurt man. You ought to let me go to a hospital."

"I think I hear the police ambulance now," said Max McGraw with satisfaction. "You're on your way, Matthews. And I hope I'll never see you again."

"Don t worry," said Zeke morosely. "When I get out, I'm heading for South America. There's too many busybodies in racing today for my taste." He looked at Monty and Julie. "Weren't for you two," he said, "and Spire, that crook, I'd be on the way to makin' my fortune. I hate meddlers!"

Then they came in with a stretcher and took him away.

Chapter 15

Monty looked at his watch. "Half an hour since Homer took off," he said. "I've got to phone Mr. Tolkov."

"Use my office," said McGraw.

They all went there, Julie objecting on the way that Monty showed no concern whatever for the poor Princess, alone out there somewhere with the murderous Homer.

"I *am* concerned, Julie, but this is all part of the plan, and I don't think there's much chance that he'll do anything stupid till he gets his hands on both horses. Now just come along like a good girl and—hey, where were you tonight? I was worried sick."

"I fell asleep. I never meant to. But I was beat."

"I thought you'd been kidnapped."

"I thought Bonnie'd been horsenapped."

"It's been a tryin' time all round," Stash said. "Be glad to see morning."

"Why'd you take Bonnie to Deepwater, if you were going to use Star Princess for a decoy?" asked Julie. So many questions had been answered tonight that she could not bear to have the few loose ends of the mystery flapping. "What's going to happen now?"

"Wait till I talk to Mr. Tolkov, Julie. Then I'll explain on the way." Monty dialed a number. Max

McGraw flipped a switch, with the young man's permission, so that the voice at the other end of the wire came out of a box on the desk, and they could all hear both sides of the conversation.

Mr. Tolkov's familiar tones filled the office, full of chuckling mirth. "The pigeon has gone for the bait, sure enough. I had a call from friend Homer a few minutes ago. He says that he's been worrying about Star Princess—and *that* far, I believed him—because she has a cough. He's running scared, Monty; he ought to know I'd have heard of it if she had! So he thinks it best to take her to Florida for the winter racing circuit, where the sun and salt air will improve her health. Now surprise, he heard tonight that he had to go down there himself on family business. So if one of the men will bring the Princess in a horse van to (let me get that address) the Blue Grass Trucker's Haven on Highway Forty, just south of the turnoff to Deepwater, by ten thirty, Homer will take over from there. I said that was fine with me."

"Great. We can make it easily. Is Bonnie in the van?"

"Bonnie?" squealed Julie, aghast.

"Being put aboard now."

"Homer has a gun with him," said Monty, ignoring her. "He wounded Zeke Matthews with it."

"Glad you mentioned it. We'll take precautions. So long," said Tolkov, and rang off.

"You're letting them take *Bonnie* to Alex Homer?" Julie said, incredulous.

"He'll think Bonnie is the Princess, just as he thinks the Princess is Bonnie."

"But he wants to get rid of the Princess," she gasped. "And if he has them mixed up, then—"

"No, no! His next move has to be to switch the fillies, to save his hide. His scheme's gone wrong, so all he can do is bring his ringer here. Then Tolkov has the real prize filly and you have the double, and he's at least managed to get out of the whole mishmash without going to jail."

"Wait a minute," McGraw put in. "He drove off leaving a wounded man here. He panicked. He can't replace a horse in a stall at Kandahar, which will be swarming with cops and owners, as far as he knows; that empty stall will have been spotted. Homer must realize that shooting Zeke messed up his deal even worse than it already was."

"That didn't occur to me," said Monty slowly. "We'll have to keep mighty close watch on him after we've made contact."

"Because he *has* to shoot his ringer," Julie said, turning very pale, "and as far as he knows, that's Bonnie!"

Stash nodded to Monty. "Julie's right. Let's move. No harm in bein' early."

Monty whistled. "Julie's car—and fast!"

"Good luck," said Max McGraw; but he was talking to a suddenly empty office.

They drove quickly away from Kandahar Park and down Route 40 as fast as the law allowed. Julie was too deeply afraid to ask more questions or to voice her terrors: Suppose we have a flat tire? Suppose he gets away?

Suppose . . .

She tried to turn off her mind, but it leaped from one terrible possibility to another. She had great faith in the two men with her, and Rollin Tolkov was a figure of power in the background, but wherever she looked she saw the cold, scarred, handsome face of Alex Homer. And he was always sighting down a gun barrel at her Bonnie.

Tolkov had said, "We'll take precautions." But it may not have occurred to him that Bonnie was in real peril.

Why did they have to bait the final trap with dear Bonnie?

Sunk in misery, she sat in the corner of the front seat and did not even notice it when Monty said,

"There's the Deepwater turnoff now. Truck stop ought to be here somewhere."

"Up ahead on your right," said Stash. "Blue neon sign."

They pulled into the Blue Grass Trucker's Haven and parked the car on the extreme northern edge of the big lot, where shadows would camouflage their faces behind the windshield. Julie became aware that they'd stopped. She blinked at the neon.

"We made it. What time is it?"

"Ten twelve. We ought to see if he's here yet," said Monty, "but he probably spotted you this morning at the track, Julie; and I don't know whether he saw me or not, that day I sent him the message at Bowie. Stash, how about scouting the place?"

"Man with a scar, in a big green this-year's Chrysler. Right." Stash slid out of the car and strolled toward the diner, carelessly glancing left and right.

"Monty."

"Yes?"

"Why couldn't they have stopped Homer at the gate of the track? He had the Princess."

"Exactly. And there was no reason under the sun why he shouldn't have had her. He could have pointed out that her tattoo showed she belonged to his employer. No case. Even with two identical fillies with the same tattoo—how could we have proved anything on Homer? We didn't know," he added bitterly, "that he was going to shoot Zeke. Or that Zeke would spill the whole story. So we had to set it up like this. Don't despair, Julie. We're going to keep on his rear bumper until he stops to put Star Princess in the van with Bonnie. Then we'll jump him."

"Won't that be here?"

"No, he'll have parked the trailer somewhere out of sight. He won't want the man who brings Bonnie to see him with a second horse."

"But . . ."

"What?"

"Gosh, I don't know. I'm scared."

"Me too," Monty admitted. "But we'll win, Julie, honestly we will. It isn't just us against him, it's Tolkov and all his people too."

Julie did not feel comforted at the thought. In the eerie blue glow of the enormous neon letters, the half-empty parking lot with the garishly painted diner at its center looked to her like a stage set for the last act of a tragedy.

Well, she thought, gathering all the bravery she could find and dropping it around herself like a pathetically thin raincoat to keep out the terror, there's no earthly use in wallowing in panic at something that may not happen. I've got to be bold and act as if losing Bonnie were the last thing I'd think of. That's what Monty's doing, for my sake; so I'll do it too, for his.

"Say," she said, "I didn't have any supper. Nor anything to drink since lunch. I'm dry as old bones."

"Here comes Stash. If our villain isn't here yet, you can scoot over to that cola dispenser by the diner and get us a couple of bottles. Here's some change," he said, "get three."

Stash sat down and closed the door. "Not here," he said.

"Right back," said Julie, and headed for the vending machine. She bought three bottles of cola and uncapped them. She turned to go back to the car, and a green Imperial came in across her path from the highway, scattering gravel from its tires. Julie hardly needed to look at the driver to know that he would have a white scar shining on his cheek.

Alex Homer swung the car in a half-circle and brought it to a halt directly between Julie and her goal. She shrank back behind the soft-drink machine, clutching her opened bottles as though they had been weapons. She was below the overhang of the roof here, in shadow, but lit weirdly by the reflected blue lights above. She twisted around so that she was looking over her shoulder at him. Homer turned off his engine and leaned forward. Was he staring at her?

No, he was lighting a cigarette. Julie walked away, trying to impersonate a local teen-ager who had never been near a racetrack. How does one of them walk? She slouched, wishing she had braided her long bright blond hair, or cut it off short, or tucked it into her shirt. Passing the front door of the diner, she scurried along and out of sight at the far end.

Going at a trot, she rounded the next corner and headed down the back of the building toward their car. She stopped and stuck her head out slowly; there was no roof jutting overhead here, and she would be plainly visible if he were looking in her direction.

He had left the automobile and was standing in front of it, hands in the pockets of his light tan overcoat. He was sweeping the lot with his eyes. She dodged back. He was unlikely to come back here unless he had seen her. She waited breathlessly. Then she said to herself, Stash and Monty know where I am, they've seen *him*, and they won't let him do anything to me here. Let alone all the truckers and other drivers who'd come in for snacks and a rest from the highway, of whom four or five were always coming and going across the parking lot. Julie cheered up. The worst that could happen would be that he'd see her and try to run. Then—why, they'd call the police, and leave the rest up to them, instead of playing detective like this!

Julie drank half a bottle of cola in several thirsty gulps. She peeked out and Homer was still there, watching the road, his back to her.

To reach the car directly, she'd have to cross the open space no more than twenty feet from him. And the gravel was noisy.

She drank the rest of her cola and set down the empty. Heading for the back of the lot, keeping the diner between them, she walked as quietly as possible to the extreme edge, cut right, and went straight across to the far north end. Then she proceeded down toward the highway till she reached the car, and got in.

"Man!" said Monty.

"Nice work," said Stash.

"Oh wow," said Julie. "That was close." She gave them their drinks. They all sat watching Homer, who paced back and forth beside his car.

"Ten twenty-six," Monty announced. "Any minute." After a while he said, "Ten thirty-five.'

"Bonnie's late," said Julie, only a little quaver in her voice.

"Here she comes."

A horse van came bumping in from the highway; Homer flagged it down. The girl and her firends leaned out of the windows, straining to hear, but the distance was too great. The driver was getting down, talking to Homer. They both went to the green Imperial and talked for a minute longer. Then the man got into Homer's car and backed it and turned to the road.

"Goin' back to Deepwater," Stash murmured. "Up to us now."

Homer was taking off his coat. He tossed it into the cab of the van. Then he walked around to the side door, cracked it open, and peered back inside. Evidently satisfied, he settled himself in the driver's seat and closed the door.

Monty turned on the ignition and started their own car. The engine turned over and coughed and died. "Come on, don't be a drag," said Monty nervously. He turned the key and gassed it and it started up again, sputtered, then caught. He glanced at the moving horse van, then down at his own lighted dashboard. "Oh oh. Julie, didn't you fill her up today?"

"I never thought to. Why?" Her breath was stuck in her throat, a jagged lump of hard air.

"That wasn't your gas," Stash said, "that was your battery, just a mite run down. You're okay now."

"I hope so," Monty said, his mouth a grim line in

his blue-lit face. "But the needle's right on Empty, and I don't think it budged when I started her."

"You mean we-we're out of gas?" Julie asked.

"The engine's movin'," said Stash with authority. "Don't borrow trouble. Get on his track!"

"Should we stop for a gallon or two?"

"No time," said Monty. He rolled out on Route 40, with one car between the horse van and themselves. "We can't lose sight of him. Everybody concentrate on the gauge being wrong."

"Think good thoughts," said Stash. In the tense and ominous atmosphere, his tone was hollow.

Chapter 16

They traveled three miles on 40, then bore right onto a smaller road. At this time of evening, there was little traffic on it. Monty, with no other vehicle between him and Homer, dropped back a hundred yards. He wished he could turn his headlights out. This was a poor way to trail a man in secrecy, with two enormous lanterns, on a dark night. But there were fewer and fewer lights from motels, diners, and drive-ins, and he could not have seen the road. He widened the distance another fifty yards.

"You'll lose him," whispered Julie.

"Don't want him to spot us."

They ascended a long hill. Homer's van went out of sight over the crest. Monty speeded up. At the top, he was just in time to see Homer's taillights flicker between trees and vanish.

"He's turned off the road. Did you see it?"

Julie said, "Yes. I'm watching where it was."

"Sing out when we get near it."

"Soon. Here!"

Monty pulled off and saw a narrow dirt track running in and twisting out of view among thin-trunked trees, a patch of woodland. Slowing the car to a crawl, he made the turn from the shoulder of the road onto the rutted track. He started into the trees. The engine hacked quietly and gave up the ghost.

"Out o' gas," said Stash. "Got a flashlight, Julie?"

"In the corner back there, a big one." She tore open the glove box and clawed into its contents, found her father's rechargeable electric torch, and tumbled out of the car, urging them to hurry. Monty had turned on the overhead light while Stash searched for the other flash. When they had located it, on the floor, he turned and looked through the windshield to see Julie reach the extreme limit of the car's bright beams, click on her small torch, and turn a bend into darkness.

"Oh, Julie!" he shouted, automatically switching off the headlights and opening his door. "Wait!" He went out head first, lost his balance on the lumpy road, and fell to his knees. "Where's your flashlight?" he yelled to Stash, struggling up and feeling his way to the front of the car.

"The batteries are dead," said Stash in a dull voice. "Lucky there's a moon. Where's Julie?"

"Way up ahead. I can't see a thing."

"Follow my footsteps." He heard Stash move ahead of him at an easy dogtrot. Monty blundered after the sound, batting his eyelids furiously to accustom his sight to the blackness. Somewhere in front, Stash said, "I hope to goodness that li'l child notices we ain't with her, if she come up with Homer first. That's a man makes no distinction between grown-up crooks and girls, if they're in his way. You can tell that to look at him. Keep close, Mr. Monty.'

"Right behind you," Monty said, and ran into a tree.

Julie was running through a nightmare. The thin weak beam of her flash, meant only for close illumination, went before her through the ghostly tree trunks, washing their bark and the black dirt road with pale yellow splashes as her hand moved jerkily back and forth while she ran. Probably because she had been breathing shallowly ever since Kandahar Park, her wind was giving out and she gasped hoarsely. She could not hear a thing except the pounding of her feet and the labored panting. She had thought that Homer's van was still moving when she first leaped away from their crippled car, for a low throb was in the air beyond her; she knew that she could not have heard it now until she came right up to it, because of her own noisy breathing.

She had to reach the van before he opened it, led Bonnie out, walked into the trees, took out the gun . . . She had to be there, with Stash and Monty. She could not hear them, but they must be right behind her. They should have caught up by now, in fact; she should see the bigger flood of their flashlight beside her, ahead of her. Maybe they couldn't keep up with her because their love for Bonnie was less intense than hers. No, they would have run their hearts out for Bonnie, she knew that. They must be just behind. She'd made a flying start, but she was a sprinter and Monty was a router—he'd catch her soon.

The road dipped and swerved away and her light, growing dimmer, barely showed her the direction it took. She was getting used to the milky moonlight, though. How far had she run? It must be half a mile by now. She could not tell. She only knew that she had to get there in time. No hysteria, no panic gave her the wings on her feet: simply love. Her horse was ahead somewhere. In terrible danger. She had to save Bonnie.

She ran through the trees like quicksilver down a tilted glass tube. She was drinking the chilly air in painful gulps. It was deep in the woodland here, and she was running alone and she knew it. Something had happened to Stash and Monty. She couldn't turn back to help, though; they were two grown men, and Bonnie was a horse who could not defend herself against a man she'd had no reason to fear before tonight.

Julie was alone and the nightmare rode her shoulders, screeching, and she was not afraid.

But a tired body will only answer on command for a certain limited time, and it began to come to her that she would soon have to rest.

She wouldn't rest. She would, if she had to, run her heart out.

Bonnie—

There was a light ahead.

Julie clicked off the almost useless flashlight; moon-light was enough now. Carrying it by the thin leather thong, realizing that it was the only weapon of any sort that she had, she ran on, staggering with exhaustion.

The light grew brighter. She turned a bend and lost it for a moment—the wood was thicker here—then saw it glowing just ahead. She drove herself the last hundred yards and reached a small clearing among the trees. The Deepwater van was there, its headlamps blazing out toward the dirt road; beside it, braced up on blocks, was the horse trailer.

Alex Homer had opened the latter and led out Star Princess, who he believed, of course, to be the Bold Ruler filly. Holding her by the halter, he had led her down to earth and to the back of the van, where he'd looped a rope through the throatlatch and twice around a branch to keep her secure while he opened the van to load her aboard. He was just reaching for the first catch that held the ramp.

Julie cried hoarsely, "Stop! Wait!" and floundered clumsily toward him, reaching out both arms. Homer whipped round and shot out his hand, fending her off.

"How'd you get here?" he demanded, obviously rattled. "You're that crazy kid from Ohio, aren't you?" He shoved her backward. "Oh, brother," he said in a desperate, choked voice. He had plainly had all the complications his nervous system could stand for one night. Probably he had been worrying himself half-sick over what to do with the ringer, ever since he had shot Zeke Matthews at Kandahar Park. "Get away from me," he snarled, pushing her back as she came at him again. "You want to get hurt?"

"You can't do anything to Bonnie," panted Julie.

She swung the flashlight hard at the end of its thong. More by luck than aim, it smashed against the back of one outstretched hand, and he howled angrily and stepped back a pace, shaking the fingers with pain. "You want to get hurt?" he roared again. "Get away? Go home! How'd you get here, anyway?" Then he dodged in and caught her wrist with one hand, and with the other gave her a vicious slap across the face, so that she fell back, lost her balance, and sprawled on the ground. Star Princess pulled away from them, tugging at the rope and whinnying with fear. Homer turned back to the van.

Julie had lost the flashlight. She got to her feet, shaking her head, and without a thought launched herself at his tall form, shrieking like an aroused Fury.

Alex Homer fell to his knees, flailing at her and cursing incoherently. She clung to his back, one hand gripping him by the hair, the other clawing at his face. She was battling by instinct, intent on preventing harm to her horse . . . to both horses. He was not a man to her, he was Evil. As her nails raked across his cheek and nose, he bellowed with rage and shook himself violently. Julie lost her grip and fell, jerking his head and overbalancing him, too. Something thudded on the packed dirt between them; it was the Colt revolver. Before he could see it, Julie grabbed it and rolled free.

She could not get it into her grasp properly. Homer struggled upright, wheezing wrathfully, and came toward her. She was on her knees, fumbling with both hands at the weapon. She had no idea of how to fire it, and wouldn't have done so anyway, but it was a marvelously effective discouragement if only she could manage to hold it correctly. Then it slid comfortably into her right palm and she thrust it up at him, the long silencer almost touching his chest. With an inarticulate squawk, he stopped in his tracks.

"Back up," she hissed at him with all the breath she had left. He retreated promptly, his face pallid in the moonlight.

"Watch out, you brat, that's a loaded gun!"

"I know it," she said huskily. "Keep backing. There, stand there."

She had found the trigger guard with her forefinger and slid it gingerly inside, not touching the trigger.

When he glanced at it, he apparently thought she was on the verge of shooting. "Take it easy," he said, "that's a double-action."

"I know it," she repeated, without the faintest notion what *that* meant. "Just stand there while I load the Princess in with Bonnie."

"That's not the Princess, you young fool."

"Oh yes it is. You're the one who got fooled." She rose to her feet and went to the van, shaking with terror; if he rushed her, she could not shoot him. Maybe she'd try to club him with the wicked thing. She unlocked the van using her left hand, keeping the gun aimed at the man. Homer showed no signs of coming at her. He must have thought she was crazy through and through.

"Well, I'll be blessed," said the mild voice of Leon Pitt above her, "doesn't look like we were needed after all." He stood at the edge of the horse van, staring first at Julie and then at the cowering Homer. A shotgun, which Julie later learned was empty but brought along as a threat, was cradled in his arms. "Hi, Julie," he said, hopping lightly down.

"Hi, Leon. I didn't know you were in there." Her voice quavered out of control. She handed him the revolver thankfully.

"Guess I didn't have to be. Here's Mr. Tolkov, too," he told her, gesturing. Rollin Tolkov got up from the bale of straw on which he had been perched and got out beside them.

"Hello, Miss Jefferson," he said weakly. He leaned on the van, wiping his face with a handkerchief. "Did you ever ride in a horse van? In the back?"

"Why, yes," she said blankly.

"This is my first time. And my last. If I have to *walk* home."

Leon chuckled sympathetically. "Mr. Tolkov maybe got a little seasick."

"I just came along to see the fun," said the bearded man in plaintive tones. "How was I to know it bounced like that?" He looked at his trainer. "Caught with the goods, Alex. Plenty of witnesses. I don't know how long you'll spend in jail, but it ought to be quite a stretch."

"I can explain everything, sir," said Homer.

"So can I," said Julie. "Better than you can, I bet. Oh wow," she exclaimed, putting a hand to her aching head, "did you ever sock me!"

Leon glared at him. "Not my practice to hit people," he said quietly, "but if you wasn't already captured, I'd be most pleased to knock you down ten or twenty times, big strong man."

Julie approached Star Princess, who was still stamping and rolling her eyes, trying to free herself; she had been terrified at the violence. "There, there, sweetheart, you're okay," said the girl gently. The horse slowly calmed down as no one else moved. Julie unwound the rope from the tree bough and led the filly up the ramp, to fasten her securely in the stall next to Bonnie.

Then Stash and Monty jogged into the light of the van's lamps and stopped dead to stare at the three men and the girl there.

"You just missed the last act," said Julie. Then the strain and fear and relief hit her, and she sat down on the edge of the van and allowed herself the luxury of a good cry, as Bonnie whickered with concern in the background.

Chapter 17

She fed Cissy and Joey, and as the pair of tawny retrievers pitched into their breakfast, she poured coffee for her father and sat down to her own cereal. Burglar got onto his lap, looking a little anxious, as though he knew what was happening.

"Then what?' Rand asked. He had been sitting on the brink of his chair, listening eagerly, like a small boy being told an adventure story.

"Leon drove the van out to the road, with Mr. Tolkov in front and everybody else in the back. Monty siphoned gas from the van into the car, and we all went to Deepwater Farm. They called for the police to come for Homer, and Mr. Tolkov says that probably they won't need me at the trial, but Monty will have to give evidence—"

"He'll have to go to Kentucky again?"

"Well, he'll be there already."

Rand laughed and leaned back, fondling the raccoon's big white-fringed ears. "Sorry, I'm pushing you ahead of your story. I won't interrupt again."

"That's all right, that came next anyway. We were all sitting around in the plushiest living room you ever saw, Dad, with milk and petit fours and tea and macadamia nuts and all that fancy stuff that millionaires eat all the time, I guess; and Mr. Tolkov offered Monty Alex Homer's job. Monty was sort of flabbergasted.

He said Mr. Tolkov didn't know what kind of trainer he was, and Mr. T said Oh yes he did, not to forget he'd been checking up on Monty and me pretty thoroughly, and Leon Pitt had said that Monty'd earned a fine reputation already as a good hand with horses. Mr. T—everybody calls him that—Mr. T said he had to have a trainer he could trust, and he didn't know anyone he'd trust farther than Monty after the fracas about Bonnie, unless it was me. And after all, I wasn't a trainer. So Monty said he'd have to check with St. Clair and his father, and Mr. T said did he have a contract, and Monty said No, and Mr. T said he was of age, then, and could just darn well come out with his own answer, couldn't he, and Monty said he guessed so, but he liked it here.

"So Mr. T said, 'Look, son, I don't usually bull my way around overbidding on the personnel I want, even if I sometimes do with horses. But I need you and money's no object.' And Monty said, 'It isn't with me either, sir, if I have the horses I want to work with and the right conditions, and the freedom to put my own ideas into practice.' And Mr. T said, 'You'll have all that, I'm sure, and for one item, you'll have a four-hundred-thousand dollar filly under your care,' and I just about died. He was going to keep Bonnie!"

"We'll fight that," said Rand darkly, "don't worry."

"You're getting ahead of me again," Julie grinned.

"Sorry. Go ahead. Would you get me some coffee, honey? I'd do it, but Burglar's *so* comfortable here."

"Sure. So: Mr. T said Leon had been telling him a lot about Fieldstone Farm, you know, where Bonnie was born; and earlier that evening he'd put in a call to Bill Morehead, who's in charge of it since Mr. Bradley died, and the upshot was that he was going to buy Fieldstone, because he's collecting such a string, and wants to go into breeding too, that Deepwater isn't big enough for his operations.

"Leon Pitt's coming out of retirement, and he'll be the foreman at Fieldstone, which he says is just like coming home. He says he has a couple good years left in him, and Mr. T says a couple, ha, at least twenty; and if you'd seen Leon then, you'd know Mr. T was right.

"Everybody was quiet for a minute and then Stash said to Monty, 'Don't pass it up; Leon knows more about racing than anybody this side of Man o' War. It'd be like getting a double salary.' So Monty said he probably would, but he'd think about it some more."

Julie poured his coffee. "Then Mr. T turned to me and looked very serious, 'cause I think he could see I was feeling awful, and he said, 'Miss Jefferson—' and I said everybody in racing called me Julie, trying to be funny. He laughed and said, 'Julie, about Bonnie.' I tried to smile at him, but I must have made a mess of it. He said, 'You know, I'm legally entitled to her, of course, but morally she belongs to you. You rescued her once, and tonight makes twice. Because even if we hadn't been in that van, you'd managed to beat Alex Homer at his own game single-handed. It's plain from what I saw when we put her in the stable that she believes the sun rises and sets on you. So she's your horse. All I ask is that she's allowed to race in the Deepwater colors. And when she eventually retires to my breeding farm, you and I will go partners in her foals. How's that?' "

"So Bonnie's still yours. Well. That's a happy ending for sure. What's Monty decided?"

"He told Mr. T he'd come with him if he could bring his own assistant trainer along. Mr. T said fine."

"Who's that?"

Julie drank some milk and stared down at Cissy, who was trying to slay her bedroom slipper under the impression that it was a large orange-and-blue mouse. "Well," she said slowly, "that's me."

"For heaven's sake," said Randolph Jefferson. Then he smiled. "Tolkov okay that?"

"Oh, yes, he said Monty's word was law if he was going to be his trainer. And he said he'd be happy to know that three honest people, Leon and Monty and I, were working for him."

"You don't seem overjoyed at the idea."

"Dad," she burst out, looking up at him, "I can't leave you all alone! I said no."

"That is sweet, but plain silly," he told her.

"It's not! I couldn't bear the thought of you, all desolate here with only a couple of dogs and a raccoon!"

"Which is why you decided not to go to college."

"Yes."

"I knew it was, even though you never admitted it before. That's why I had your name entered for scholarships at a couple of places before you got Bonnie."

"You *did?* I had no idea," said Julie, gaping.

"Then you were so happy, and went to work in earnest for Will Everett, and I canceled the requests, because I think, I very soberly and firmly think, Julie, that you were born to work with horses; and four years of college wouldn't do much to further that career unless you went into veterinary work. But as for leaving me, you have to, sooner or later, don't you?"

"No! Why should I?"

"Because you have to make your own life, dear. I hate to sound corny, but all birds leave the nest when they can fly; and wolf cubs grow up and make their way alone; and colts and fillies go to the track without their sires and dams. Agreed?"

"But you—"

"I'm not the most helpless and forlorn of men, Julie, whatever my daughter happens to believe." He smiled at her. "You and I have been friends, as well as parent and child, for a long time. But these relationships don't end simply because the child grows up and leaves home. You grew up in my eyes when you waded into a river to help a suffering animal. I knew it was only a matter of a little time till you'd go into the world with your banners flying, either to work or to marry. That you'll be going with Monty, as trustworthy a fellow as I know, cheers me up remarkably; and that you'll be working with horses doesn't surprise me in the least."

"But I——"

"Oh, yes, you are."

"I am?"

"You just made up your mind. I helped. No matter how far away you are, honey, you're still my daughter and friend. Fillies may lose track of their mothers, but girls needn't ignore their old dads because of a few miles between them. I have the store, my pals here, a good companion I've recently rediscovered in Will Everett, and plenty of work, the kind I like best. The kind *you* like best is waiting in Kentucky. So that's where you're going."

"You won't get so lonesome you'll d-die?"

He laughed heartily, and Burglar got up in disgust and jumped to the floor, where he batted Joey on the nose and crawled under the stove. "Good heavens, what a weak critter you must think I am! No, dear girl, I won't. I'll be fine. And I'll visit you often. Now go and tell Monty you're his new assistant."

She looked at this grand and kindly man for a long moment. Then she stood up. "You're super, Dad, you know it? All right, I'll take Mr. T's job. And I'll visit you, too. And everybody will be happy."

"Yes. Especially, I think," he said, taking her hand, "our little bay filly Bonnie."

The End

Ⓞ

SIGNET Books You'll Enjoy

☐ **EDGAR ALLAN by John Neufeld.** In this penetrating novel, John Neufeld examines the problems that arise when a white middle class family adopts a black child.
(#Y6628—$1.25)

☐ **LISA, BRIGHT AND DARK by John Neufeld.** Lisa is slowly going mad but her symptoms, even an attempted suicide, fail to alert her parents or teachers to her illness. She finds compassion only from three girlfriends who band together to provide what they call "group therapy." (#W8775—$1.50)

☐ **FOR ALL THE WRONG REASONS by John Neufeld.** From the bestselling author of *Lisa, Bright and Dark* comes a tender, taut novel about a teenage marriage that speaks of today.
(#E9146—$1.75)

☐ **SUNDAY FATHER by John Neufeld.** The touching story of a young girl's painful adjustment to her parents' divorce.
(#W7292—$1.50)

☐ **TWINK by John Neufeld.** The hopes, failures and courage of a young girl with cerebral palsy who could have been forgotten, and wasn't, and how love and touching and caring made the difference in the face of an almost overwhelming physical handicap. (#W9145—$1.50)

SIGNET Young Adult Books by Phyllis A. Whitney

- [ ] THE HIGHEST DREAM — (#Y6552—$1.25)
- [ ] LINDA'S HOMECOMING — (#Y9004—$1.50)
- [ ] A LONG TIME COMING — (#Y9310—$1.50)
- [ ] MYSTERY OF THE ANGRY IDOL — (#Y8435—$1.25)
- [ ] MYSTERY OF THE BLACK DIAMONDS — (#Y8612—$1.50)
- [ ] THE MYSTERY OF THE GULLS — (#Y7798—$1.25)
- [ ] MYSTERY OF THE SCOWLING BOY — (#Y7530—$1.25)
- [ ] MYSTERY OF THE STRANGE TRAVELER — (#Y7588—$1.25)
- [ ] MYSTERY ON THE ISLE OF SKYE — (#W9151—$1.50)
- [ ] NOBODY LIKES TRINA — (#W8275—$1.50)
- [ ] SECRET OF GOBLIN GLEN — (#Y7420—$1.25)
- [ ] SECRET OF HAUNTED MESA — (#Y7913—$1.25)
- [ ] SECRET OF THE SAMURAI SWORD — (#W9155—$1.50)
- [ ] SECRET OF THE SPOTTED SHELL — (#Y7468—$1.25)
- [ ] STEP TO THE MUSIC — (#W7531—$1.50)
- [ ] WILLOW HILL — (#W9535—$1.50)
- [ ] CREOLE HOLIDAY — (#W8224—$1.50)

Buy them at your local

bookstore or use coupon

on next page for ordering.

SIGNET Dictionaries for Your Reference Shelf